ICE

A novel by
Renée Perrault

ISBN-13: 978-1512259018
ISBN-10: 1512259012

Chapter 1

Jeffery Andrew Zamboni was a retired NHL star, known to his friends as Ice, or sometimes "The Cleaner," because his name was the same as the machine that cleaned the ice rink at half time. A multi-millionaire at twenty-eight years old, even with a few scars from his hockey days, he was still definitely eye candy. With dark hair and smoldering brown eyes, he was what the female fans called the "Italian Stallion." That was the problem. Ice loved women, all women. He changed girlfriends like most people changed television channels. He was honest with all of the ladies; a long term relationship was not in the cards. Most of the women were content just to be seen with a former National Hockey League star and the biggest philanthropist in town. This system of serial dating worked until he hooked up with a hot model named Connie Razzini. He mentally dubbed her "Crazy Connie." After two dates she tried to talk commitment to a man who hadn't had three dates in a row with the same woman since high school. When Crazy Connie realized date number three was the final one, she took action. After telling Ice he was the only man for her, and she was very sorry he didn't feel the same way, Crazy Connie shot him at point blank range.

Fortunately for Ice, Crazy Connie shot him during dinner at a restaurant right across the street from a hospital. Even better, a trauma surgeon was seated at the table next to them. Location, as they say, is everything. Ice was rushed into surgery and then put into a medically induced coma to help his body heal. However, there was a minor glitch during the surgery and Ice was heading toward the bright lights.

***

"Damn, turn out the lights. This is the worst hangover I've ever had."

"Jeffrey Andrew Zamboni, wake up. Wake up now."

Where the heck was he? Was he flying on a plane? He felt like he was flying. Ice opened his eyes and immediately wondered if someone had slipped something into his drink. He literally saw an angel, but not just any angel. This one had a cigar in his mouth and if you ignored the halo and wings, bore a strange resemblance to his uncle Tony.

"Come on kid, wake up. We don't have much time. It's me, Uncle Tony. I'm supposed to give you a choice. Stay up here with us or go fix your life."

"Uncle Tony? What's with the wings? Wait a minute, I can't be talking to you, you're dead, and I recognize the polyester leisure suit we buried you in. No offense Uncle Tony, but I really hoped to never see that suit again. Is this Hell and you have to wear it for eternity? Besides, I'm not dead. I can't be."

"Hey, don't be a wise ass. I love this suit and I think the style is coming back. Forget about my suit; we need to talk about you. You're not dead but only because they owe me a favor upstairs. Well, technically we are "upstairs." I mean the guys over in procurement. Those angels screwed up big time when they took me.

I was supposed to have another twenty years but they pulled me up early. So, now they owe me and it's a good thing for you 'cuz I'm gonna get you out of this mess."

Uncle Tony sat back and puffed on his cigar. "Now, let me tell you one thing Ice. It hasn't escaped the big Guy's notice that you are--well, technically it's called being a man whore, but we don't talk like that up here. Let's just say, the man whore thing would have landed you down south asking for a lighter shovel. The good news is you have always been a generous guy. Even as a kid you'd always ask your mom to make an extra sandwich to take to school for someone in need. You've spent a lot of the money you've made as a NHL player for the good of your community. Believe me kiddo, it's the only reason you're getting a second chance."

"Maybe they grabbed you because of your suit. Uncle Tony, what do you mean second chance? I can't be dying. Why would you think that? Wait--Crazy Connie shot me. Did she kill me? Is this what being dead is like? Damn."

"Son, first of all, language. Remember where you

4

are. The big Guy don't take to the bad language so much. And, in the second place, you're wrong. To state the obvious, you're DEAD wrong. Well maybe not yet but you're failing fast. They nicked an artery getting the bullet out. Right now you're pooling up with blood and there's not much time. So answer me this….do you want to do a good deed and see if we can turn this all around?"

"Uncle Tony I don't want to die, I've got too much going on in my life.

"Son, I've been watching you. You don't have much going on that means anything important. You're twenty-eight, no wife, no kids, and you don't stay in touch with your family as often as you should. You need to listen to me and get your life back on track. And, in order to stay alive, you need to do a good deed to make up for something you did a long time ago."

Ice looked at his uncle. He knew exactly what Uncle Tony was referring to.

Chapter 2

10 Years earlier

Ice walked next door to his best friend's house. He and Sheri McLellon were neighbors; they'd known each other since they were born. Sheri was the only friend he could tell anything to. She was also his polar opposite. Ice struggled with his grades and Sheri was the smartest student in the entire school.

Without bothering to knock, Ice walked in the back door. He looked at Sheri sitting at the kitchen table, her nose in a book. "She dumped me for a frat boy."

Sheri looked up from her book, pushed her glasses up and tried to figure out what Ice was talking about. "Who dumped you?"

"Jeez, McLellon, try and keep up. Tiffany dumped me. She was my prom date. Prom is in two days. Do we really go to the same school or do I just imagine it?"

"Watch it Ice. Are you talking about head cheerleader Tiffany Martin with the IQ of a guppy?"

"No need to get mean about it. You're supposed to console me; I'm your best friend."

"You need to buck up and get a grip. Are you going to let her stupidity ruin your prom? You're on the ballot for Prom King. You have to go."

Ice, still inconsolable, said, "Sure, I can buck up but that doesn't get me a prom date. Now who am I going to prom with?"

Sheri cut to the chase. "It's your choice, you can stay home and sulk or you can invite your best friend to prom."

Ice looked at her in disbelief. "I've been listening to you for four years talking about how lame the whole high school experience has been. Now you want to go to prom?"

Sheri looked the dumb jock in the eye and said, "You could do worse you knucklehead. What? You want to sit home and let her win?"

Ice thought about it and knew she was right. "OK, you're on. We'll go to prom and show the shallow bitch she didn't get to me."

***

Sheri was flying high. The day before Prom night she got her braces off. To celebrate, her mom took her out for a new haircut and makeover. Feeling like a caterpillar coming out of her cocoon, Sheri was pretty pleased with her transformation. Keeping her head in the books had given her a 4.0 GPA and a big zero everywhere else in high school. Being the smartest student in school, Sheri hadn't really been concerned with her looks. For prom, she wanted just one Cinderella night rolled into one memorable high school event. And maybe, just maybe, the knuckleheaded jock she had a huge crush on would finally look at her.

Her mom called up to her from downstairs. "Sheri, Jeffrey's on the phone."

Sheri's mom was the only one in the state who refused to call him by his nickname.

"Okay, mom, tell Ice I'll be right there." Laughing

because she knew her mom had made a face at the name Ice.

Picking up the phone Sheri had a huge smile on her face. "Hey, Ice, what's up? Are you having problems picking out my corsage?"

Ice shut his eyes and the words rushed out. "I can't take you to prom. Tiffany called. Her frat boy dumped her for a keg party and she was in tears, begging me to take her."

Sheri's eyes widened in disbelief. "You're telling me that you're cancelling our date? Oh, wait, let me look at the clock....an hour before prom you're cancelling?" Sheri's voice rose and she held the phone in a death grip.

Ice squirmed on the other end of the phone. "Well, I did ask her first and I know how you hate this sort of thing so I thought it would be okay."

Struggling to keep her voice calm, Sheri paused before she spoke. "Sure, Ice, I don't see how it could not be okay. I bought a new dress, had my hair and make-up done and I've been getting ready all day. You just go ahead and comfort poor sad little Tiffany and don't worry about me."

Ice hadn't heard the sarcasm dripping from her voice when he responded. "Thanks. You're the best. I knew you'd understand. I'll see you tomorrow okay?"

Sheri didn't bother to respond. She exercised her remaining self-control and managed to place the phone back on the cradle without slamming it.

Two days after graduation, Ice was drafted for the Colorado Avalanche League and left town. Sheri ignored all of his phone calls and refused to see him when he came to her house to say goodbye.

By the time Sheri left for college, she was still wondering how a 4.0 honor student could have been so blindsided. Vowing never to put herself in a vulnerable position again, Sheri refused to get involved with any of the young men who noticed her brains and beauty. She decided she would never make herself vulnerable again. No one was ever going to get close enough to trample her heart again.

Chapter 3

Ice thought back to the worst moment in his life; losing his best friend. Sheri had always been such a brainiac and he really thought cancelling their date wouldn't matter to her. He had been such an idiot. Acting like a typical seventeen year-old boy, thinking only with the small head.

"Kid, if you decide you want to do the good deed and stay alive, you'll be seeing her soon. She doesn't know it but she's in danger and about to make a huge mistake. You need to stop her."

"What kind of mistake Uncle Tony? I don't even know where she is or how to find her." Ice stared at his uncle, trying not to be distracted by the halo and wings.

"OK, kid, it's settled. I'll be watching over you and I'll fix the nicked artery problem with the docs. Oh, one other thing. A minor detail really, nothing you can't handle. The big Guy…who knew he had a sense of humor? Remember all the times the ladies you broke up with called you a low-down dirty dog? Well son, payback's a bitch."

***

Ice woke up from the strangest dream he'd ever had. Whoa, what's with the tongue? Crazy Connie was waking him up porn star style. Turning over and opening his eyes, Ice screamed when he saw a set of Rottweiler balls directly overhead. He heard a furious bark and realized it came from him. Scrambling to get free he pawed his way out from under the big dog. Looking around, Ice saw he was in a park but he had no idea where.

"Hey, mutt, what's with the attitude?" The Rottweiler growled and snapped his enormous jaws in the air towards Ice.

***

Sheri McLellon was enjoying a beautiful sunny fall day in Seattle. She loved living in the Northwest and found Seattle, and all its charming little neighborhoods, perfect for her small town roots. Each neighborhood was like a small city and made the city, as a whole, less intimidating. As she walked around Green Lake, a popular park north of downtown Seattle, she spotted a big dog picking on a little Chihuahua.

"Get away from that poor little dog. You heard me, get away." Sheri's voice was firm. "You big bully, leave the tiny dog alone."

Tiny dog? Ice looked down and saw two tiny paws and when he sat down saw hind legs, a tail and--*whoa, what's with the micro balls? I'm a dog? I'm a frigging dog? What the hell happened? Either the big Guy really does have a strange sense of humor or I'm in the middle of another weird dream.*

"Come here little fella. You poor thing." Sheri McLellon scooped up Ice and cuddled him up to her face. "Look, you're shaking. That big bad dog must have scared you to death. Poor baby."

Ice looked into eyes he hadn't seen in over ten years. Sheri McLellon had matured into a beautiful woman. Some light laugh lines creased her eyes and he knew the serious young girl had turned into a woman with a sense of humor. Warm green eyes smiled down at him and his heart melted. He noticed her curly red hair was long and free of the traditional pony tail she used to wear.

"You don't have a collar and it looks like you've been on your own for a while. You're pretty scruffy." Sheri looked at the dog and smiled. "I know a place that finds homes for strays. Let's get you there and see if you're micro chipped. We'll find your family little guy."

As Sheri cuddled the dog, a tall man dressed in a hoody ran straight at Sheri, yanked her purse from her arm, and ran towards the trees. Ice jumped out of her arms and chased the thief. Although he wasn't too pleased with his high-pitched barking, Ice kept running until he was finally able to grab the purse-snatcher right in the ass. Biting for all he was worth, he heard the guy scream a long litany of curses.

"Let me go ayou frigging dog. Let go."

As he screamed, a well-dressed man appeared. Surrounded by trees with no one else around, Ice was relieved to see help arrive.

"Get this guy; he stole my friend's purse. Get him." Ice realized words were not coming out of his mouth, just frantic high-pitched barking.

The well-dressed man gave Ice a hard kick sending him to the ground. He then turned to the robber. "Damn it, Roger, can't you get anything right. This was supposed to be my moment to shine as her rescuer. Hurry up and put the bug on her phone. I'm keeping track of this pot of gold."

Ice sat stunned and took in the scene. He continued to bark at the two men as the well-dressed man took the purse from the Roger. "Now get lost. I'll tell them I tackled you and got the purse back but you ran off."

"Yeah, great plan Trevor. Last time I draw the short straw. This is total bullshit. I should be the one getting close to her and you should be here with a dog bite on your ass."

"Roger, this girl is worth millions. Her great-uncle just died and left her a fortune. I need to get in on the ground floor and get access to her bank accounts. Hopefully, I can get close to our little Miss McLellon and transfer her funds to my account in the Grand Caymans. It would be so sweet to be set for life."

"Trevor, you're an asshole but if this works, you'll be a rich asshole and that's something I can live with, especially when I get a cut of the loot. Meet me at my place later and we'll use the chip in her phone as a transmitter to keep tabs on who she talks to and where she goes." Roger put his hands to the back of his pants and tried to pull his hoody down to cover the hole as he ran up the hill to his car.

Ice continued to bark and snarl at Trevor. "Hey, cool it dog. I just saved her purse." Laughing, Trevor started down the hill to begin his charade.

***

Sheri McLellon screamed and was about to run after the robber when a man rushed towards her. "What happened? Are you okay?"

"A guy grabbed my purse and ran into the trees. A dog I just found chased after him."

"I'm Detective Warren Trimble with the Seattle Police Department." The man took out a badge and flashed it at Sheri. "Can you give me a description of the man?"

"He was running towards me, not unusual on this

path with the traffic lanes for runners and bikes. I just rescued a dog being attacked by a Rottweiler and wasn't really paying attention. He had on a black hoody and sunglasses, slight build, about six feet tall. I'm 5'10 and I think he was a little taller."

As Trimble was about to go into the woods, a man came out of the trees carrying a purse. Ice was circling the man, barking frantically. Trevor put on his best face.

"Is this yours? I was standing up the hill when I saw the guy grab it and your dog take off after him. That's one brave little puppy. He might be a little sore; I saw the purse-snatcher give him a pretty good kick. I started chasing the guy, and between the dog and me, he dropped the purse and took off." He paused and gave Sheri his most charming smile as he held out his hand. "My name's Trevor Long."

Sheri McLellon looked up into the bluest eyes she had ever seen, long eyelashes she would kill for, and a smile with teeth so white she was almost blinded. She noticed his deep dimple and her mind started to take her to fantasy land with the handsome stranger in a starring role. Tapping down her hormones and composing herself, she smiled back. "Thank you for rescuing my purse. I sound like a cliché, but it all happened so fast."

As she was speaking, Ice decided to take advantage of his new body. Lifting his leg, he let a stream of urine soak the creep's Gucci loafers.

"Oh no, I'm so sorry. Stop it!" Sheri reached down and picked Ice up. "This isn't my dog, in fact I'm taking him to a shelter to see if he's chipped and try to find his owner."

Detective Trimble struggled to keep a straight face as the dog peed on Trevor's shoes. The guy was too smooth and got on his nerves. Who comes to a park dressed like a male model wearing Gucci shoes? He wanted to take a statement and ask the very attractive Sheri McLellon out, but before he could, the dog started barking again.

Ice was staring at the policeman, "Hey dude, arrest this guy. He set this all up. Damn it…..why don't you understand me?"

Detective Trimble leaned over and petted the dog in Sheri's arms. "This little guy is pretty protective of you, Miss McLellon. If he doesn't have an owner, you should keep him."

"Oh no, I don't think so. I'm too busy for a dog."

Trevor interrupted. "I know a family that is looking for a puppy. Why don't I take him?"

Over my dead body, Ice thought to himself. He looked at Trevor and let out his most ferocious growl. Trimble was growing very fond of the dog. "He only seems to be happy when he's with you."

Ice wagged his tail and licked Sheri's hand, anxious to get out of there before Trevor put some moves on her.

Trevor turned on the charm again and gave her another killer smile. "I know I'm being a bit forward, but I'd love to see you again. Maybe we could go out for coffee, or better yet, dinner tomorrow night?"

Sheri blushed, feeling like an awkward teenager. She thought Trevor was very attractive and it had been ages since she'd been out on a date. Her green eyes lit up with pleasure. "I'd love to, as long as you let me treat you to dinner. It's the least I can do for rescuing my purse."

Oh jeez….she's falling for this guy's bullshit. Ice was trying to figure out how to get her out of the situation when Detective Trimble coughed.

"I don't want to hold you up, Mr. Long, I'm sure you have somewhere important to be so let me get your statement and we'll let you be on your way."

This ought to be good. Ice was barking furiously, *"He knows the guy…he set it all up."*

Sheri looked at Ice as she said, "Another reason I can't take this dog with me is he barks too much. It would drive me nuts."

Hearing that, Ice stopped mid-bark. He looked up into her face and whimpered. He gave her a tentative lick on the face and looked as pitiful as he could. Not too hard since he was muddy and scrawny looking.

Trimble scratched his ears. "See, he understood you. He stopped barking immediately."

Trevor did not like how this was going. He had to get the mutt out of the way so Sheri would focus only on him. "I'll be happy to take him to my friend's house. I'm sure they'd give him a good home."

Sheri looked into the dog's dark eyes and kissed

the top of his head. "No, thanks anyway, I'll take him to the shelter and see if he's chipped." Digging into her purse Sheri pulled out a business card and handed it to Trevor. "Thanks again for saving my purse. I'm serious, I owe you dinner. My life is in my purse. If he'd gotten away with it I would have been devastated."

Trevor smiled and read her card. "You're a sportswriter? You must meet a lot of interesting people."

Sheri gave a rueful laugh. "Most of my girlfriends are so envious that I meet with jocks all day long. It's not as glamorous as you would think. Players have huge egos and sometimes they don't like what I write about them. Plus, most of them don't like talking to female reporters."

Trevor had done his homework and knew she worked at The Seattle Times. "Wait a minute, I've read your stuff. You did a great interview with our star quarterback from the Seahawks. You're good!"

Sheri blushed. As an insecure writer, she craved praise, but it always embarrassed her. She looked at Trevor and gave him a big smile. "It's nice to have feedback from a reader." Looking at her watch she turned to Detective Trimble. "Let's finish the report now. I need to get to the shelter before I go to work."

"Sure. No problem. Mr. Long, we're finished with your information. Ms. McLellon, let's go sit over there and finish up the report. Effectively dismissing Trevor, he walked Sheri over to a picnic table and sat down.

"I just need to get some contact information from you. I'll keep you in the loop if we find the suspect."

Warren Trimble smiled at Sheri and for the first time, she actually looked at him. He looked like classic cop until a killer smile transformed his face. His blue gray eyes were twinkling and a straight nose and even white teeth made for an attractive face. Thinking to herself, girl, you have been dateless too long. You're starting to fall for every guy you see. Sheri tried to get her mind back on track to business "I'm sorry Detective, what were you saying?"

"This is a bit awkward, but I was just wondering if I could take you to lunch or dinner tomorrow? It's my day off."

Caught off guard, Sheri was at a loss for words.

"Oh, well yes, that would be nice. Lunch could work, as you just heard I have dinner plans. Wait, this isn't a ploy to sell me tickets to the Policeman's Ball is it?"

"Miss McLellon, Seattle Cops don't have balls." Instantly his face turned bright red. "I mean, we do have balls just not formal balls." Looking at Sheri as she could barely hold back her laughter, he went on to say, "You know what I mean."

"As we say in Minnesota, "Ya sure, ya betcha."

"Minnesota. You're a long way from home. How'd you end up in Seattle?"

It's the farthest I could get from Minnesota and you don't have a national hockey team. I wanted to be a sportswriter, not interview a bunch of dumb ice jocks who have been hit with a puck one too many times. Too many hockey players in Minnesota."

Ice looked at Sheri thinking, *Ouch, I think she still has some resentment going….dumb ice jocks?* He watched as the shy cop tried to think of something else to say. *Great, now we have a tongue-tied cop with no balls, a con artist with big balls and me, a dog with the tiniest balls in the universe. This is a mess. How the hell am I going to save her?*

23

As Ice was watching Sheri and Warren make goo-goo eyes at each other, he spotted his Uncle Tony standing a few feet away. "Uncle Tony, what are you doing here?"

"Hey kid, I told you I'd be keeping an eye on you. Is the situation under control?"

"Gee, I'd have to say no on all counts. She plans on dropping me at a shelter. Me...the Ice Man! It's humiliating. I'm doing my best to be adorable but, seriously, a Chihuahua? Why not a Golden Retriever or a Labrador....you know, a smart, good looking dog?"

"I told you Ice, the big Guy has a sense of humor. Just hang in there and for Pete's sakes, stop scratching. She's gonna think you're some south of the boarder flea bag."

"Great, friggin fleas probably have bigger balls than me!"

Chapter 4

Sheri stopped at the shelter and was dismayed to find out the little rat dog was not chipped. A volunteer looked at her and said, "If you have it in your heart, you need to take this one home. We have Chihuahuas coming out our ears. The rich and famous made them the "purse dog of choice" and people went nuts buying them. Then, when they were too much trouble, the dogs got dumped at shelters. We just got twenty shipped up from California. I've got to tell you, it doesn't look good and, to be honest, they are way cuter than this sorry looking thing."

Ice snapped and growled at the man and tried to bite him thinking, *I'll show you cute.*

"Hey, calm down. Honestly, he's been kind of sweet except he doesn't seem too fond of men." Sheri struggled to maintain hold of a pissed-off Ice.

"We get that sometimes. If an animal has been abused by a male, it takes a long time for the trust to come back."

Ice looked at Sheri and whined. Looking down at the pathetic little thing, she weakened. "OK, we'll try this out but you'd better be on your best behavior at my house. I'm telling you....one problem and you're out."

Ice barked twice to say thank you.

Scooping him up, she put Ice back into her large purse. "Let's stop at a pet store. If you're going to be a purse dog you need some outfits."

Ice groaned. He hated shopping and didn't want to think about what kind of outfits a purse dog wore.

As Sheri turned to leave, the volunteer called out. "By the way, looks like he hasn't been neutered. You'll have to take care of it before he gets too much older. Snip, snip."

The dog let out such a painful yelp Sheri had to laugh. "Hey little guy, it's almost like you knew what he was saying."

***

Sheri picked up her cell phone and hit auto dial.

"Johnni, it's me. Listen, I have a situation going on and I have to cancel tonight."

"No way Jose…you are not canceling. You're the one that always complains you never get dates. Girl, we are getting you a date with some fine man tonight if it kills me."

"Johnni, right now it is raining men. My purse was snatched while I was at Green Lake and a very handsome man rescued it by chasing the mugger. He asked me out and the cute cop who took the report asked me out. And if I want to make it a three-peat, I've got this damn dog that turns out is a male, although it's hard to tell."

"You've got a dog? What kind of dog? You can't have a dog with you know who. I want to hear all about it tonight. You are not cancelling!"

Knowing when to throw in the towel, Sheri finally just said, "Fine, call me later with details."

***

Pulling into a parking spot by PetSmart, Sheri got out of the car and headed to the front door. Immediately assaulted by barking dogs, she saw it was "Adopt a Dog

Day." Looking at the fenced dogs in the center of the floor she noticed, of the 20 or so there, over half of them were Chihuahuas. Looking down at her new purse dog she said, "The Shelter guy was right. Looks like there are a lot of abandoned Chihuahuas. Today is your lucky day."

By the time they left PetSmart, Ice had a new bed and a collar with enough bling to make Lady Gaga jealous. Sheri also outfitted him with two new outfits and a purse with a mesh window on one side so he could have a view. He actually was kind of excited about the purse. *Man, look at me. My teammates would laugh their asses off if they heard I got excited over a purse. Plus, I'd never live it down if they saw me now, as a scrawny mutt in a plaid sweater with a studded collar. Damn, it's not even a kinky collar.*

Sheri pulled up to her house and turned into her driveway. Before she hit the remote to open her garage door, she stopped the car for a moment and surveyed her front yard. A mid-century home on a small lot, the yard had a beautiful maple tree currently a glorious shade of orange. Fall was her favorite time of year and the yard was filled with color as the trees changed from green to yellow, orange and red. The scientific side of her thought about the wonders of photosynthesis. Sheri was proud of her house and all the work she had done in the five years she owned it. She had painted every room and totally remodeled the kitchen with granite counters, new cabinets and stainless steel. The kitchen was her dream come true and allowed her to indulge in her love of cooking. The outside of her home had traditional wood clapboard siding painted a light grey with dark blue and maroon trim around the windows. It was a warm and inviting home. Sheri thought of it as her sanctuary to hide from the craziness of the big city of Seattle, so different from her hometown in Minnesota.

Once the garage door closed, Sheri opened the door into the house. Ice went into full investigative mode. Running from room to room, barely noticing the décor until he ended up in Sheri's home office. Looking at the wall-to-wall bookshelf, he noticed numerous pictures of Sheri's family. On the bottom of the shelf was an old picture of Ice and Sheri, wide smiles on their sunburned faces, holding fishing poles and a string of good sized fish. Ice stopped and stared at their smiling faces and for a moment he was absorbed in his trip down memory lane. *I remember that day….it was great. We sat out on the dock all day fishing and talking and arguing about football teams.* In his excitement, he knocked the picture over. Hearing the noise Sheri came into the study just as Ice was licking the picture and wagging his tail.

***

"Oh no, I totally forgot about this picture. Great, you have to fall in love with the jerk who broke my heart." As she leaned down to pick up the framed photo, Ice gave her hand a tentative lick.

"What a sweet puppy you are….yes you are…poor baby. I didn't mean to get mad, it's okay." She cuddled the tiny Chihuahua. As Sheri held him, there was a feral sounding meow coming from another room. "Uh oh, the beast is awake. Come here Cleopatra, come to momma."

Cleopatra was a large Maine Coon cat that weighed twenty pounds, and, at least ten of it was fur. She was a big- boned girl with long multicolored grey and black fur. As she sauntered into the room the cat stopped five feet from Sheri. Sitting down, she waited for Sheri to come to her. When she noticed the scrawny little dog in her arms, Cleopatra let out an accusing meow. *"What the hell is that creature supposed to be and what is it doing in my house?"*

Sheri looked at her cat. "Well Miss Cleo, we have a new roommate. I'm going to put him down and you be nice." Placing Ice on the floor she squatted next to him.

Ice looked at the cat. *"Holy shit moley, she's huge. She's the fattest cat I've EVER seen. Looks like she's never missed a meal. If there is a Jenny Craig cat food, she needs it."*

Cleopatra looked at Ice and let out a very feral sound just before leaping in the air and landing on him. *"Fat? You just called me fat? Oh hell no! Listen you scrawny, flea bitten, gross, teeny tiny useless little dog, I run things around here and you are not staying. I'm bigger than you are, I'm smarter than you are and oh, way better looking, so don't start thinking you're 'all that.'"*

After digging her claws into his back, Ice was horrified when she sat on him. *"Wait, you can understand me? You heard what I said?"*

"Of course you idiot. Cats have excellent hearing. Really, ours is better than dogs. We just don't let humans know because then they expect us to come when we're called, and that just won't do."

"If you can understand me then get the hell off me. You're suffocating me with all your fur and I'm allergic to cats." Aaaacccchhhoooo. *"See, now you've done it. And me without my inhaler."*

"Allergies, are you nuts? Only humans get allergies."

"Yeah, I know. And that brings me to my other problem."

***

Sheri sat and watched the cat and dog. Both were emitting weird sounds and growls to each other. If she didn't know better she would have thought they were talking, but that's impossible. They were probably both trying to stake their claim to the house.

"OK you two. All three of us are going to co-exist, and that includes getting along. First order of business, we have to name the dog."

Cleopatra took a look at Ice. *"Oh please, let me, let's see...he's a Mexican Chihuahua....how about Estupido?"*

Ice looked at the cat. *"You speak Spanish?"*

"*Of course I do. I'm home alone all day. What do you think I do, sleep? When the owner's away, the cat will play. I'm either on the computer or doing yoga. What do you do...make burritos?*"

"*Computer? Am I supposed to be impressed because you can work a mouse? What's your favorite position in Yoga, The Downward Dog?*"

As the two animals snarled at each other, Sheri blurted out "Pablo." That's your name. Come on Pablo, let's get you bathed. Maybe Cleopatra will like you better if you aren't so dirty and smelly."

Chapter 5

Trevor Long loved technology, at least the parts of it he knew how to use. Sitting in his dingy apartment he could hear every word Sheri said. *Man, the bug Roger planted on her phone is powerful. I feel like I'm right in the middle of her house. This is going to be like taking candy from a baby.*

Roger walked in the door carrying two bags of groceries. "Brought some junk food, need to keep our nourishment up."

Trevor laughed, "We're not going to be at this too long. I already heard a phone call between Sheri and some chick named Johnni. They're going out tonight and, oh, what a coincidence, I'm going to run into her. The minute we figure out where she's going and when, you need to get into her house. We need to get her bank account number and dig around for a password. I plan on transferring her 3.8 million dollars to an account in the Cayman Islands within the month. You can get in without breaking a window or anything, right?"

"Yeah Dude, no sweat. Her keys were in her purse and I did a wax impression of her house key and had a copy made. We don't want to tip her off with a break in."

"She still has that damn dog, so watch out. For a small little mutt, he really has an attitude."

"Shit, tell me about it....notice I'm not sitting down. My ass is killing me. That dog will meet with an accident if he comes near me."

Trevor looked down, "Yeah, well he didn't pee on your shoes. I paid a fortune for these Gucci's! Dog's got a death wish."

***

Sheri finished bathing Ice and put him back in the plaid sweater and studded collar. As she cooed over him, Cleopatra hissed. *"Hey, Estupido, don't get too comfortable."*

"Back off you overstuffed hair ball. I'm here to help Sheri and I'm not leaving until I do. She's in danger and I'm stuck in this damn body until I fix it." Ice glared at the cat, knowing

she outweighed him by about 12 pounds and had really sharp nails. He was scared to death of her.

Uncle Tony decided to pop in. Cleopatra's tail fluffed up to twice its size and her green eyes dilated. She looked like she was ready to kill a rodent. *"Oh my God, look at that suit. You've got to be with Estupido over there."*

Despite himself, Ice laughed. *"You're right, meet my Uncle Tony. Tony, this is Cleopatra and watch out for the claws. She's meaner than a junk yard dog."*

"See Ice, you still don't understand females." Uncle Tony piped in. "In the span of two minutes you've called her fat and mean. That just don't work with the fairer sex. You've got to use charm and appreciate them. Right honey?"

"Hey, your uncle is right. Now stop scratching and tell me what's going on."

Ice gave her all the details he knew. Cleopatra shook her head. *"I know why. She's been really quiet about it. The only one that knows is her best friend Johnni. I heard her on the phone with the lawyer and then a few days later she came home crying. An uncle she barely knew left her over three million dollars a few weeks ago. I always sit on the desk when she's working, and she's been downloading charities like crazy. I think she intends to make quite a few donations with the money."*

Ice looked at Cleopatra and his uncle. *"Sounds like her. She's the one who made me grow a conscience. When we were kids, Sheri always shared whatever food she had with anyone at school that needed it. That's why I always asked for an extra sandwich and gave it away. My mom just thought I was hungry because I was growing so fast."*

Cleopatra hissed at Ice. *"Hey, you better do something or this money is going to get her killed. How does this Trevor guy even know about it?"*

Ice growled and thought he would like to bite her in the ass and take out a chunk of fur. Then he remembered his allergies, and decided to just give her his patented scathing look. Something about being a Chihuahua, the look didn't faze her. *"Someone must have told Trevor. His name is Trevor Long, I wonder what her uncle's attorney's name was?"*

"Well genius, it would be easy enough to find out. She keeps the papers in her desk drawer. Oh, I forgot, you don't have thumbs. Kind of hard to open a drawer without them."

They both looked at Uncle Tony. "Hey kids,

sorry, but I'm only here as an advisor. I can't physically do anything to help you." Lowering his voice he said, "I'm an Angel and we have thumbs but we're more like ghosts. You can see us but we're not solid. Thumbs don't work unless you're solid."

"Oh for Pete's sake, you two are pathetic. Watch this." Cleopatra went over to the desk where Sheri sat. She rubbed and rubbed against the drawer and did her most charming meow.

"What do you want Cleo? Did your toy get dropped in the drawer?" As Sheri pulled open the drawer, she heard her cell phone ringing in the living room and got up from her chair.

With Sheri out of the room, Cleopatra purred with her tail all fanned out and swishing back and forth. *"OK boys, you can come in now. I was purrrfect. I swear an Academy Award is in my future."*

Ice went over to the drawer and looked at the file headings. A tab marked "Will" caught his eye. *"OK Cleopatra. Can you snag this file with your claws and pull it up?"*

"Remember, I'm helping Sheri, not you." Snagging the file, she pulled it up half way. Ice stuck his head in the

file and tried to read.

"*Damn it....that son-of-a-bitch. The lawyer's name is Marvin Long, obviously related to Trevor. He must have told Trevor about the will.*" Ice was having a meltdown.

The cat made a noise that resembled a laugh. "*Interesting term, 'son of a bitch.' You do know it's ironic when you say it, right?*"

"*Can you just try and stay on track for a minute? We need to find out about Marvin Long. Come on, get your big fat cat ass back over here and help me push this file back down.*"

Cleopatra's tail fluffed up and she snarled, "*Excuse me. You want my help, be nice.*"

Ice realized males of all species had to put up with female's crap. It was something he would have learned long ago if he'd ever had more than three dates with the same woman. It was time for some of the charm that got him voted as People's Sexiest Man. "*Cleopatra, I'm sorry. I'm worried about Sheri and taking it out on you. I actually like cats. I would have one but it's the allergy thing.*"

"*Estupido is a perfect name for you because you are stupid. You don't "have" a cat, we have you.*" Cleopatra was speaking very slowly. "*Now Sherlock, I have a plan.*"

***

Sheri picked up her cell phone and glanced at the caller ID. "Hey Johnni, what's up?"

"Girl, we've picked the spot. We're meeting at The Zodiac Bar on 45th and we'll head to Ballard for dinner after we do happy hour."

Sheri thought about trying one more time to cancel but abandoned the idea. She knew from experience her tenacious friend would not take no for an answer. "Okay. But I'm only doing this because I know you will hunt me down and kill me if I back out. What time?"

Johnni laughed. At six foot one, she was a stunning beauty. Her mahogany skin was flawless and with her aristocratic features, she looked like an African Queen. It was easy to see why she was a top model, with a face you saw on magazines at the checkout line of the grocery store. Johnni was her own "Brand" and she worked it well. Her sense of humor is what made her and Sheri perfect friends. "Girl, hunting you down would be too easy. I'd just sit at the flannel pajama section of Target and you'd wander in eventually. I keep telling you to spice it up a little. Be there early. I told everyone 5:30 but get there at 5:00 so we can talk. I want to hear about these two guys you met, and I know you won't talk in front of the others."

"Ok, see you at 5:00." Sheri hung up the phone and started thinking about what to wear.

***

Ice and Cleopatra called a truce. After figuring out the scum- bag lawyer was somehow related to Trevor, they came up with a plan. Ice would play purse dog tonight to keep an eye on Sheri. They figured since the phony purse snatching had been staged, anything could happen.

He had three hours before they would go meet Sheri's friend so Ice continued snooping around the house. He was curious about the kind of woman Sheri had grown into. Knowing she was generous as a child, and Cleopatra confirmed she was as an adult, Ice wondered about her life now. Obviously she was single. Looking in her home office the walls were lined with awards and pictures with some pretty influential sports figures. He laughed to himself when he saw there were no hockey pictures. He looked at the shelf with her CDs. It was as he expected: Michael Buble, Josh Groban and a lot of 80's rock. Figures she'd go for the crooners. She'd had a mushy side when we were kids.

Ice wandered into Sheri's bedroom. It had gold walls with white trim and the dark mahogany sleigh bed had a maroon and gold bedspread with lots of decorator pillows on it, feminine but not frilly. Everything was neat and looked well organized. It was a comfortable room. Sniffing around, Ice jumped when he saw himself in the mirror in the master closet. His only thought was, *the guy at the shelter was right. I am one ugly Chihuahua.*

***

As Ice sat in the closet looking at his reflection, Sheri came in and started digging through her wardrobe trying to find something "Johnni Approved" to wear for their night out. Sheri and Johnni met their freshman year of college. Johnni was a Seattle native attending the University of Washington on a scholarship to study Marine Biology. Johnni was the total package: brains, beauty and evil sharp humor. When she spotted her new roommate dressed in baggy jeans and a flannel shirt,

Johnni was convinced Sheri was gay. Johnni kept introducing Sheri to various lesbian friends. Sheri finally figured it out and with an embarrassed laugh, told Johnni she appreciated the effort but wasn't gay. From that moment on, Sheri was Johnni's "project." She critiqued her clothes, even throwing some of them out the window of their second story dorm room. Johnni's constant refrain to Sheri was, "You're not in Minnesota anymore. You can't dress like some back woods fisherwoman. We're going to accentuate all the good stuff you've got going on. From now on, girl, you are my personal Barbie doll."

Sheri drew the line at dressing like Barbie, but by the end of their senior year she had a wardrobe of clothes that worked for her coloring and active lifestyle. The little caterpillar that blossomed for the aborted senior prom date blossomed again. She was now a gorgeous young woman with a natural distrust of the opposite sex. She'd had one boyfriend in college and her introduction to sex had left her knowing that he wasn't the one. After that, if sparks didn't happen by the third date, she moved on. Had she known that Ice had the same three date rule, she would have been chagrined.

Sheri picked a sleeveless black dress with what she considered to be a plunging neckline and what Johnni would consider one step from a nun's habit. Laying it on the bed she walked into the bathroom to get ready.

***

Cleopatra wandered into the bedroom and jumped on the bed. *"Oh, I thought so; it's a little black dress night. I love black dresses."*

Just as she was about to lay on the black dress and deposit a pound of cat hair, Ice wandered in and let out a howl.

Sheri came out of the bathroom. Ice turned away from Cleopatra and found he was looking at a very naked Sheri. He let out a yelp and laid on his back in the submissive position.

"Oh little boy, you just want someone to dominate you don't you?" Sheri scratched Ice's stomach.

Ice did all he could not to stare up at her naked breasts. It made him feel like a pervert, a very lucky pervert, but a pervert nonetheless. When he started to get a familiar tingle in his lower regions, Ice was embarrassed. Glancing down, he was beyond mortification. Wondering, with this type of equipment, how were Chihuahuas even made?

When Cleopatra made a noise, Sheri's attention was diverted to the cat. "Cleo, get away from my dress. I swear you are a black dress magnet. You're the reason 3M makes billions a year on sticky tape. Get away. Oh, Cleopatra, you got the dog's outfit full of cat hair."

Ice stood up and just when he thought he couldn't be any more humiliated, he saw his "outfit" on the bed next to the dress. It was a little bow tie with a shirt and vest. If dogs could blush he would be bright red. *Good God, I'm going to look like a doggie Chippendale dancer. This is sick.*

As Cleopatra was shooed off the bed, she sauntered past Ice. *"Oh, sorry, hope your allergies don't get to you with all the cat hair on your spiffy little outfit."*

Ice was about to chew the outfit to little pieces but just as he was making the jump, Sheri came out for her dress. Wearing a thong that disappeared into her backside and a sexy black bra, Ice was overcome with desire. *Jeez, now I understand why dogs hump human's legs. It's a compliment.*

***

"OK, Pablo, it's your turn. Come here." Sheri grabbed Ice and, despite his struggling, managed to get the one piece outfit on him. "You look adorable. Go show Cleopatra. She'll be so jealous."

Ice jumped out of her arms and went under the bed. As he was contemplating his next move, his nemesis appeared. Two green eyes stared at him and he thought he heard the sounds of laughter. Cats don't laugh do they?

"Hey Estupido, you look good enough to eat. In fact, you're about the size of the last rat I brought home. It was disgusting, but occasionally I feel the need to contribute to the household. Come here little doggie, let me take a nibble."

Ice decided being stuck under the bed was not a position of power. He tried a maneuver that always worked on the ice. He feigned left and ran like hell to the right, shooting out from under the bed and running straight into Sheri's arms. Looking up at her smiling face, Ice realized how much he had missed his friend and sincerely regretted being a foolish shallow jock that was just looking to get laid on prom night. He should have realized Sheri was the real thing.

***

Walking into the Zodiac Bar, Sheri looked for her friend. She had Pablo in a black bag with a mesh side. He had a bird's eye view of the place and noticed quite a few heads turning as Sheri walked by.

Sheri spotted Johnni and made her way over to the table. Johnni already had two men buzzing around her like bees to honey.

"There's my girl. You two go away for awhile. I need to catch up with my BFF." Johnni swatted at the men like they were flies. "Ok now spill. What's going on with you?"

Sheri settled into her chair. She placed her purse between her and Johnni. "What a day. All I wanted to do was take a walk around Green Lake and look at the beautiful fall leaves. The purse snatch thing brought on all sorts of crazy. I ended up giving my phone number to the guy who saved my purse and to the cute cop. Then, to top matters off, I'm now the not-so-proud owner of a Chihuahua. Take a look."

Sheri opened the top of her purse and Ice poked his nose out. "He's not much to look at but he seems to have a pretty good personality. He's very protective of me, which is funny, considering I've only had him for about eight hours. He and Cleopatra have a love hate relationship, but I'm sure it will get better."

"Oh look at him, he's so tiny." Johnni started to reach into the bag to pull Ice out.

"Don't take him out. They don't allow dogs in here unless they're aid dogs and there is no way anyone is going to believe that. I had to bring him. Cleo's eyeing him like he's dinner." Sheri patted Ice on the head and shut the purse. She made sure he had a good view and went back to her conversation. "Trevor, the guy who saved my purse, is pretty cute. He asked me out to lunch or dinner. I think we're doing dinner tomorrow night. He asked me right in front of the cop, who, once Trevor was gone, asked me to lunch for tomorrow. Jeez, no dates in months, and now two in one day?"

Johnni looked at her best friend. "Listen to you. You are the Goldilocks of dating. You're always like,

'This one is too old.' 'This one is too young.' You never find the one that's 'just right.' Or you hate their job, or their car, or their mother. No one is asking you to settle for someone who is not right for you, but at least give some of these guys a try. If nothing else, you'll get a meal and, hopefully, some pleasant conversation."

Sheri waved the waiter over. "I'll have the house Chardonnay. Johnni, you doing the usual?"

"Oh, hell yes. This has been a lemon drop kind of day. Hit me with your best."

"OK, back to your lecture, only it's my turn. I haven't felt any chemistry with any of those men. If it's not there right away, it's just not going to happen."

"Whoa girl, didn't you tell me the guy that broke your heart was your best friend? You weren't in love with him from the very beginning? You said it was a nice long friendship right?"

"You are the only one I've ever admitted to that I was crazy about Jeffrey "Ice" Zamboni. It's embarrassing. We were neighbors and best friends our entire life. One day, I think I was fourteen, it just hit me. He was laughing over something I'd said. He always laughed with such enthusiasm, like the whole world was there for his amusement. All of a sudden, I just knew I loved him and always would. That's what made it so hard when he dumped me for the cheerleader. He never saw me the way I saw him, you know, a forever kind of thing. I'm over it, really I am. It's just I haven't met anyone who really floats my boat." The waiter dropped their drinks off and Sheri took a big sip of her chardonnay.

Ice sat in her purse taking it all in and wanted to kick himself for being so stupid. Why hadn't he figured it out sooner? Maybe he was just a dumb ice jock after all.

"What about the two guys today?" Johnni was like a dog with a bone.

"They're both nice looking. Trevor is very handsome and the cop, Warren, is very cute. I was a little freaked at having my purse taken so I didn't really get a chance to talk to them too much. Now before you start another lecture, yes, I will go out with both of them, and I won't make any judgments about either one until I get to know them better." Sheri scanned the bar,

"Because the thought of spending my best years sitting in a bar looking for Mr. Right is depressing as hell."

"Oh come on, we aren't really looking for Mr. Right in bars, we're looking for Mr. Fun or maybe Mr. Well Hung." Looking at Sheri's face, Johnni burst out laughing. "That got your attention didn't it? You're so easy to freak out. Oh look, here comes Kathy and Linda. Let's just chill and see how the evening goes."

***

Trevor was at his apartment a mile away and loved hearing the conversation. "Oh, so our little Miss McLellon has a broken heart. Waa Waa. Who doesn't? But I love hearing her sad little story. It gives me plenty of ammo."

Trevor looked at himself in the mirror. He smiled at his reflection. "I do clean up nice." Having spent eight months at a minimum security prison in Oregon for embezzlement and forgery, Trevor was in great shape. He had worked out in the gym every day and his body showed the effort. He wasn't over-muscled like some ex-cons. Trevor didn't consider himself to be an ex-con, he just got a little greedy with his employer's money. It could happen to anyone.

Grabbing the car keys, he turned to Roger and said, "Don't forget, you need to call my cell in one hour so I can pretend that my buddy can't make it tonight. That should buy me some time with Sheri."

"Yeah. Will do. I'm going to head to her house now. I'll take the transmitter so if she decides to go home early I can cut out of there. If you hook up with her, it should guarantee me a few hours to go through her stuff."

"Get as much personal information as you can. I need her social security number, date of birth, and mother's maiden name. She should have tax returns in her home office. Dig around." Trevor was ticking off the items on his list. "If we get the basics, we should be able to transfer the money. This would be so much easier if I had computer hacker on my resume."

"Yeah, I hear you. I'm good with the crazy electronic gadgets but I'm no hacker either. So now you get to go drink in a bar filled with beautiful people, and I get the grunt work." Roger stomped off to go change for his break in.

***

Trevor walked into The Zodiac Sign and took a seat at the end of the bar. From there, he could see the entire bar and watch Sheri. She was sitting with three other women, all about the same age. They were dressed for an evening out and their attire suggested they were not staying at the Zodiac. Known as a retro 80's bar, the Zodiac was not fancy, but it was a fun gathering place. Most of the walls had been painted with chalkboard paint and people wrote their best pick-up lines down for posterity. As he waited for the bartender to take his order, Trevor started reading the walls.

"I was wondering if you had a band-aid? I scrapped my knee falling for you."

"Do you have a sunburn or are you always this hot?"

"I was wondering if you have an extra heart? Mine seems to have been stolen."

"Smoking is hazardous to your

health…and baby, you're killing

me!"

Trevor couldn't help but laugh at some of the lines on the wall thinking, when I'm living in the Cayman Islands, I'll have to use some of these. The bartender finally came over and Trevor ordered a glass of merlot. He glanced over at Sheri's table and figured he'd have to make his move soon or they'd be gone. He stood up and told the bartender to leave his drink since he'd be right back. He started walking towards the men's room just as he saw Sheri head to the ladies room.

Weaving his way through the crowd he kept his eyes on Sheri, intercepting her at the start of the hallway going into the restroom area. "Sheri? Wow, hello. What a nice surprise!"

Sheri looked over when she heard her name. Seeing Trevor she immediately thought stalker, and then mentally slapped herself. "Trevor, what are you doing here?"

"I'm meeting a friend. What are you doing here?" Trevor gave her the big smile, the one he practiced in the mirror each day.

"Girls' night out. We like to come here for Happy Hour. It's a blast from the past. I love all the pick-up lines from the 80's written on the walls."

"I'm new to the neighborhood. I don't live too far from here and saw a write up in the local paper. My running buddy, Brant, is supposed to meet me here."

Sheri looked him over. He seemed sincere and he was so cute. "That's great. This place has a good happy hour. We usually hit it once or twice a month."

"I was going to call you to talk about our dinner date but I didn't want to look like a stalker. I really want to take you out." Sincerity was oozing out of Trevor's pores.

Sheri looked at him and smiled. "I'd love to do dinner. Where do you want to meet?"

Trevor smiled thinking, *so that's how she wants to play it. Like I don't already know where she lives.* "Do you like spicy? I know a great Thai place in Ballard. Let's meet at the Jade Palace at 7:00 pm tomorrow. Will that work?"

"Perfect. I love Thai food, too. I'll see you

tomorrow." Sheri smiled as she walked into the ladies room.

Trevor was also smiling, thinking to himself, *yep, like taking candy from a baby*. He headed into the men's room and then back to his seat at the bar, waiting for his phone call from Roger.

***

Roger Williams looked at Sheri's house. She'd left some lights on, including the front porch light. Using his key, he quickly walked in the front door. Stopping in the entry way, he looked into the living room and saw the largest cat he'd ever seen sleeping on the sofa. Walking softly, he made his way down the hall to find Sheri's home office.

Cleopatra opened her eyes. She'd heard the door open but, thinking it was Sheri, didn't bother to get up. When she realized it was a stranger, she decided to see what he was up to before making her move.

Creeping down the hall, Cleopatra stopped just before the office door. She heard the man talking to someone.

"Yeah, I'm in the house. No, nothing so far. I'll

start digging through her files in a minute. Yeah, yeah…I know, social security number, mother's maiden name and any passwords. Oh yeah, and I've got to find her bank account number. Ok. Later." Roger opened the drawer to dig through Sheri's files.

Cleopatra started to growl and then she did an Olympic gymnast move that would have made Gabby Douglas envious. The cat vaulted over the winged back chair and landed on top of Roger's head, claws fully extended, and teeth set on kill. Roger jumped up from the desk chair and spun around, trying to get the cat to let go.

"Oww, get off me. Get off now." Roger spun in circles and tried to crash the cat into the wall.

Cleopatra jumped off and decided his ankles looked positively yummy. Getting a good hold on his Achilles heel, she chomped down until she tasted blood. She then ran out of the room, knowing the murderous sound that came out of her victim did not bode well for her.

Roger wanted to chase her down but knew it was pointless. Cats always have hiding places, and he didn't have time to waste. As he turned to continue his search, a screeching sound impaled his ears. "Oh my hell, what is that?" Roger was screwed. The burglar alarm was going off and he needed to get out of the house immediately. He went to the back door and noticed it had four windowpanes and a lock that needed a key both inside and out. He pulled out the key and prayed it operated both doors. He was just able to close and lock the back door when he heard a car pull up to the front. Seeing blue flashing lights, Roger made his way through the back yard, opened the gate, and walked into the dark alley. If he had glanced back, he would have seen a pair of green eyes watching him from the window.

***

Once he was out of sight of the house he pulled out his cell phone. "God damn it Trevor. Why do I have to be the one mauled by her fucking animals? I couldn't get any information. The damn cat jumped me and then the burglar alarm went off. I was lucky to make it out of there before the cops came."

Trevor was still sitting at the bar. "Calm down Roger. Did you get anything at all?"

"Are you not listening to me, you asshole? Maybe it's the music in the background or all the beautiful people laughing and talking. Listen up. I said THE FUCKING CAT ATTACKED ME. Did you hear that? Now I have a head that looks like pit bull's chew toy. I have bite marks and scratches everywhere. I've never seen anything like it. If I hadn't seen the cat, I would swear a Tasmanian devil just attacked me. I'm doing all the hard work here. We are renegotiating my split."

Trevor did his best to keep a neutral expression on his face. He had the phone pressed close to his ear; worried someone would hear Roger's screaming. "Just go home. I'll see you later and we'll talk."

For the thousandth time, Trevor cursed himself for not learning computers in prison. At least he might have met a hacker to help him instead of that idiot Roger. Standing up he threw money on the bar and walked over to where Sheri was sitting.

Johnni watched him approach and gave Sheri a little nudge in the ribs. "Looks like that fine man is headed your way."

"He's the guy that saved my purse. I ran into him

on my way to the ladies room." Sheri was trying to be discrete. She didn't want Kathy and Linda to hear. They too were always on Sheri about her lack of dates. The three of them were like sharks, and Sheri didn't want them to smell blood in the water.

Trevor smiled at Sheri. "My friend just called and cancelled. He has a project due tomorrow and isn't finished, so I guess I'll head for home."

Johnni took a look at him and gave him a big smile. "We're not leaving for another hour if you'd like to join us for a drink."

Trevor gave Johnni his best grin and did his shy tentative act. "Are you sure? Looks like you ladies are having a good time. I don't want to interrupt."

Kathy and Linda turned to see who the girls were talking to. Sheri resigned herself that there was no way she could get out of introducing Trevor to the group and would be totally grilled the minute he left. As Trevor was pulling a chair up, Sheri's cell phone rang. Glancing at the number, she jumped up. "Oh my God, my burglar alarm is going off. I have an auto call on my phone. I've got to go. Sorry Trevor, sorry ladies. I'll call you later." Sheri picked up her purse and practically ran out the door.

Trevor called after her. "Sheri, wait, I'll come help you."

Johnni tugged at his sleeve. "Don't bother Trevor. That is one very independent lady. She's fine." Johnni hadn't missed the fact that Sheri's new dog had practically charged out of the purse the minute he heard Trevor's voice. Even with the loud music, Johnni heard a very threatening growl come out of the little dog. She wanted to see what was up with this guy.

***

Trevor Long was trying to keep a smile on his face. Sitting here while Sheri's friend Johnni was trying to weasel information out of him was excruciating. He kept trying to turn the tables and ask about her life. "So you're a model. I bet you do a lot of traveling."

Johnni gave him her mega-watt smile, "Yes I do. What's your favorite place to travel to?"

Trevor stretched his long legs under the table. "I love Paris, I mean, who doesn't? It's the most romantic city on the face of the earth." He smiled at the memory of his last weekend in Paris, and of Marie, the sweet little French hooker who had some mind blowing drugs.

He had been steadily embezzling money from the land development company he worked for. As the manager of Accounts Payable, he set up a phony consulting company and the money just started pouring into his private account. Trevor's mistake was he couldn't help living large and letting everyone know it. Instead of quietly enjoying the money, he flaunted it. He passed it off as an inheritance from an aging aunt. This worked until the State Auditors came in to inspect the books prior to awarding a government contract. By the time the phony account was discovered, Trevor had made off with over a hundred thousand dollars. During his brief six- month crime spree, he bought a new wardrobe, had his teeth fixed, started paying $125.00 for a haircut, and flew to Europe for long weekends.

When his house of cards collapsed, his uncle represented him in court. He tried to get Trevor time in a minimum security prison and barely succeeded. The case was assigned to Judge Aaron Drew who had hated Marvin Long since law school. Marvin did the only thing he could think of to do. He had one of his young, hungry female associates sleep with the judge and take a cell phone photo at an opportune moment. To the audience in the courtroom, it appeared that the heartfelt plea from Trevor's mom swayed Judge Drew who sentenced Trevor to one year in minimum security prison in Shelton, Washington. Marvin couldn't resist giving the Judge a knowing wink.

Even in a minimum security prison, Trevor was scared to death. When an influential politician, in jail for accepting bribes, offered to help him, Trevor jumped at the chance. After six months of being at the Senator's beck and call, doing all the grunt work he didn't want to do, Trevor had almost decided that being someone's bitch in a regular prison would be easier. The only good thing was listening to the Senator brag about all the other things he had done without getting caught. This inspired Trevor to go for the big bucks next time around. And his meal ticket was Sheri.

Chapter 6

Sheri lived close to the Zodiac bar and was home within three minutes of the call. Pulling into her driveway, she saw a police officer standing in her yard. Getting out of her car, she made a beeline for the front door.

"Miss, please wait. I haven't cleared the house." The officer was right behind her. When she turned Sheri saw an older, heavyset man wearing a Seattle Police Department uniform shirt with buttons straining around the middle. When he spoke, his voice sounded like he had gargled glass. "I'm Officer Davies. Are you Sheri McLellon?"

Sheri looked at Officer Davies. The gravelly voice was offset by the kindest looking eyes she had ever seen. "Yes. Can you check the house? I really want to go in and make sure everything is okay."

Officer Davies' tone became businesslike. "Of

course you do. Ok, let me tell you what I know. An alarm was called into us seven minutes ago. The alarm went off at 5:45 p.m. I work this area and was only a few blocks away. I didn't see any signs of forced entry on either the front or back door. Your windows are all shut, but I'll have to look to make sure they're locked from the inside. If you'll give me your house key and just wait here a moment, I'll clear the house and then you can go in."

Ice was making frantic noises and Sheri thought he might need a potty break. She pulled him out of her purse just as Officer Davies opened the front door and the little dog shot through it like a bullet.

"Cleopatra where are you? Come here, quick." Ice was frantic. He needed to see the cat and find out what was going on. He heard a long shrieking meow.

"Estupido, cats don't come. You want to know what's going on, get in here. I'm in the bedroom."

Rushing into the bedroom, Ice saw Cleopatra on the bed, apparently taking a leisurely bath. *"Jesus, you fat fur ball. I was worried and you're taking a bath?"*

"I have to get the scent of that man off me. Eeeooww, he

was disgusting."

"Start from the beginning, and stop with the bath. I need to smell you and see if I recognize the scent." Ice gave her a good sniff. *"Oh man, you smell like the guy I bit in the ass. You're right, he tastes bad."*

Cleopatra snuggled up to Ice. *"You're not too bad of an ugly mutt. I think its cute how you rushed in to save me."*

Ice rolled his eyes thinking, *Women, they're the same no matter what they are.* He had to admit to himself, the thought of losing Cleopatra, the only one he can talk to right now, other than Uncle Tony, gave him a fright. He needed   a   partner.

"OK, so we know it's the same guy from this morning and Trevor Long just happened to be at the bar tonight. How'd he know?" Ice replayed the scene with the purse snatchers. *"Damn, while I was biting his ass, he had Sheri's phone and keys in his hand. I bet he put some sort of bug on the phone. He probably copied the key too."*

Cleopatra looked at Ice. *"You must be right because he used a key to get in. Sheri's not safe here."*

"I'm going to go see what the cop has to say. Stay here, I'll be right back." Ice jumped off the bed and ran back to the

living room.

***

Officer Davies completed his search of the house. "Miss McLellon, the windows are all locked on the inside, and from what I can tell, it doesn't look like anything has been disturbed. Take a walk through and tell me if you see anything out of place."

Sheri walked through each room. When she got to the bedroom she took a moment to cuddle Cleopatra. "You poor girl, I'm so glad you're safe."

Cleopatra purred, happy to see her person and wishing Sheri could understand her. *If you only knew the ordeal I've been through. It was terrible!*

Sheri walked back to Officer Davies. "Everything seems to be okay. If someone was in here, they didn't get a chance to do anything before the alarm went off. Earlier today, someone snatched my purse at Green Lake. It was recovered, but do you think this is related? Detective Trimble has the report."

Officer Davies thought for a moment. "Detective Trimble? I don't recognize the name. What precinct?"

"I don't know. I didn't think to ask. I'm sure

there's a report on file somewhere."

"I'll look into it. How long was your purse out of your control? Who saved it? Also, Miss McLellon, this could just be a coincidence and your alarm went off in error. It happens. If you only knew how many times I go to the same house because the alarms go off for no reason. We actually charge homeowners after one false alarm. Seeing how you had the purse thing earlier, I'm not going to write this up as a false alarm. My best advice to you is to get your locks changed. Anytime something like this happens, it's cheaper in the long run. Better safe than sorry. I've got a daughter about your age, and that's exactly what I'd have her do. In fact, there is a 24 hour locksmith not too far from here. I bet you could get him over here pretty fast." Officer Davies was about to leave when he felt something at his feet. "Hey, little guy, you're pretty friendly aren't you?"

Sheri looked on in amazement as Ice wagged his tail and jumped up on the Officer's leg. "Wow, Officer Davies, you must have a way with animals. I just got him and so far he's hated all the men he's met. All but Officer Trimble."

"I always say dogs can tell things about people. They've got radar. Sometimes it pays to watch their signals." Laughing, Officer Davies said, "course it's easy for me to say since he likes me. Guess I wouldn't be telling you that if he growled!"

Sheri walked the officer to the door and thanked him. Walking into her office she opened up Google to search for a locksmith and picked up the phone on her desk. After she made the appointment, Sheri wandered into the living room and found Pablo with her cell phone in his mouth.

"Pablo, drop my phone. Bad dog." Sheri reached for the phone just as the dog dropped it on the tile floor. The cover opened and a little cylinder fell out of her phone. "You broke my phone, bad dog."

Ice didn't care how many times she called him "bad dog"; he had to destroy the bug. Grabbing it in his mouth, he ran down the hall. With Sheri in hot pursuit, he raced into the master bathroom and dropped the little disk into the toilet. Cleopatra, in a rare moment of solidarity, came and sat by him as they both stared down Sheri.

"Do you think she'll figure it out?" Cleo looked over at her new friend.

"If she'd put the phone back together, it would probably work perfectly. By the way, I got a scent off the little bug. Smells like our ass guy. Oh, sorry, maybe we should call him face guy. Sounds like you got a piece of him too. Whatever. He's connected to Trevor and that can't be good."

Cleo purred at Sheri. *"So you think they were listening to her phone calls?"*

Ice remembered a woman he dated twice, Marcie Nelson. She didn't even make the three-date cut. He met her at a Starbucks when she started flirting with him. A gorgeous redhead with curly hair, she reminded him of his long lost friend Sheri. When Marcie asked to borrow his cell phone because hers was in the car, he willingly handed it over. He left the table for a minute to pick up his latte and went back to his seat. Marcie was just finishing her call and handed his phone back to him. For the next three weeks he kept running into Marcie. At first he chalked it up to coincidence, but then in conversation, she would talk about something he hadn't told her. When Ice went in to the Verizon store to upgrade his phone, the guy said, "Dude, you've got a bug on your phone." Finally, putting two and two together, it added up to Marcie. He didn't even bother asking for a third date and funny, without the bug on his phone, he stopped running into her around town.

"Oh yeah, I'm sure they were listening to her phone calls and could have been listening to her at home, too. These guys are smart for dumb asses." Ice was getting worked up again. *"As soon as I get out of this body those guys will be toast."*

Cleopatra looked at him. *"Hey Estupido, what if you don't get out of that body? What then?"*

"My Uncle Tony said I'll get back to myself as soon as I help Sheri."

"Is your taste in clothes better than your uncle's?"

***

Trevor and Roger heard a scream, "What are you doing? Not the toilet!" and then everything stopped.

"God dammit, the bug has stopped working. What the hell?" Trevor stood up and started pacing. "This has been a major screw up since the beginning."

"Well it's not my fault they found the bug. It was in the phone. Who the hell opens up their phone?"

Roger was absent-mindedly rubbing the scratches on his forehead.

"It's probably those stupid animals. Now we're working in the dark. I've maxxed out my credit card. I can't afford to buy another bug." Trevor was fuming.

**

Sheri picked her phone up and put it back together. She was startled when it rang.

Pushing the answer button, she looked at the phone number and didn't recognize it. "Hello."

"Sheri? This is Warren Trimble. How are you? Will we be able to go to lunch tomorrow?"

Sheri smiled and the song "It's Raining Men" by The Weather Girls went through her head. "Well Detective Trimble, how nice to hear from you. Yes, lunch would be great. Where do you want to meet?"

"Do you like Mexican? There's a great little place on Shilshole, right by Anthony's. It's called Maximilian's. How about 11:45? That way we can get a seat by the window. They pack in a pretty big lunch crowd. We can have lunch and then take a walk on the beach at Golden Gardens."

Sheri smiled. "I'd love that. When I moved to Seattle, the first beach I went to was Golden Gardens. It's beautiful, especially on a clear day with the Olympic Mountains in the background. I'll see you at 11:45."

Warren decided to say goodbye before he made another big embarrassing blunder in front of her. He was still recovering from 'Seattle Police don't have balls.' "Ok, I'm looking forward to seeing you."

"Me too, thanks for calling Warren. See you tomorrow."

Sheri hung up her cell phone. At least she hadn't alerted Warren to the latest police activity at her home and looked like she was some helpless female. She sat in her favorite chair and wondered what the heck was going on? What was the piece from her phone Pablo dropped in the toilet? Walking into the bathroom, she looked down into the pristine white porcelain bowl. She got out her bright yellow Playtex gloves and reached into the water. Retrieving the little round disk, she washed it under hot water and dried it. Turning it over in her hands she had a suspicion of what it was. Now the question was why?

The front doorbell rang, interrupting her thoughts. Pocketing the disk, she walked into the living room on the heels of Pablo, who was already heading to the front door.

Looking through the peephole on her front door, Sheri did an involuntary gasp. A tall Nordic God was on the other side. A bright white polo shirt was hanging in all the right places over a ripped chest that happened to be eye level with her peephole. Straining to look up she figured he must be at least 6'5". Still admiring the view, she was startled by a knock on the front door. She could feel the vibration on her side and then a deep voice announced. "Miss McLellon, I'm Peter Arnstrom from Safety Lock. Are you home?"

Breaking out of her nasty little fantasy, Sheri opened the front door. "I'm sorry. I guess I'm still a little spooked. Do you have some identification?"

Peter Arnstrom smiled, showing perfect white teeth and two big dimples. "Yes, other than the truck in your driveway with our logo on it, my shirt with a logo, and my ever ready tool box, I do happen to have a picture ID card from Safety Lock." He presented the

ID card and smiled at her. "I can understand you being a little nervous. Why don't I get started changing the locks?"

Sheri was humming the second verse of "It's Raining Men" to herself. She couldn't seem to get the song out of her head.

Absolutely soaking wet. It's rainin' men.

Hallelujah

It's rainin' men

Ev'ry spe-ci-men:

Tall

Blond

Dark and lean

Rough and tough and strong and mean.

Sheri mentally slapped herself and smiled at the tall blond handsome man in front of her. "Please come in. I'll show you the backdoor. It needs to be rekeyed too."

"Ok, let me set my toolbox down. Do you have a door from your garage with the same key?"

"Darn, I forgot about that one. New total is three

doors to be rekeyed. I shouldn't complain. It would have cost me way more if the purse snatcher had made off with my credit cards or cash." Sheri walked to the kitchen door.

"That's a shame. Where were you?" Peter Arnstrom gave her a sympathetic smile and before she could answer, Ice came running out from the bedroom. "Wow, that's the smallest dog I have ever seen. Teeny tiny."

Ice took umbrage with the teeny tiny comment but chose not to growl. Something about the guy was familiar. He took another look. Damn, it was Peter Arnstrom. Best goalie in the Canadian league. Ice had heard he was from the Pacific Northwest but didn't realize Peter lived in Seattle. Ice started jumping up and down in front of Peter, making happy dog noises. Ice was embarrassed about the sharp squeaky sound he was making but didn't care. It was good to see a friendly face.

"Sure is friendly. Shame he probably wouldn't be much use in a break in." As he spoke, Peter leaned down to pet Ice.

Sheri found herself rushing to her new dog's defense. "He bit the guy that took my purse in the butt. Sounds like he did some damage. I'd say he's pretty protective. You must be some sort of dog whisperer. He seems to like you."

Peter had a puzzled look on his face. "I usually don't warm up to little dogs. This one, as my mom always says, has a face only his mother could love. Ugly little guy, but it looks like he's got a pretty good personality. His tail is wagging so fast he might get air!"

Ice was ecstatic. He and Peter had been roommates for a year. Even though he couldn't communicate with Peter, it still felt like he had a friend to help with this mess. Ice ran into the bedroom. *"Cleo, get your bad ass out here. The guy changing the locks is an old hockey buddy of mine."*

Cleopatra stood up and arched as she let out a very loud yawn. *"Estupido, a friend isn't going to help you unless he can understand your screechy little voice like I do. Okay, I'll bite. Show me this friend of yours."*

Cleo followed Ice out. Cleo took one look at Peter and started rubbing against his legs and purring.

"Estupido, you didn't tell me he's a Nordic God. He's beautiful." Cleo continued to purr and then did her famous meow as she sat in front of Peter.

"Well look who we have here. What a gorgeous kitty. You look like you need a belly scratch." Peter leaned over and scooped Cleo up into his arms.

"Heaven, I'm in heaven and Estupido, don't you dare spoil it." Cleopatra stared at Peter and purred.

Sheri watched the scene taking place and raised an eyebrow. "Cleopatra, you are an absolute traitor and a hussy. Look at you throwing yourself at a total stranger. Honestly, she never warms up to people this fast. Did you rub catnip or chicken liver on your face before you knocked at my door?"

Peter laughed. "No, I swear I usually don't have this effect on animals. Your little dog started it and then he ran for the cat. Quite a circus you have going on here. Cleopatra is this one's name?" Looking down at the purring cat, Peter petted her under the chin. "OK, little beauty, I need to get to work. I'm going to put you down before your kitty drool gets all over me. I've seen your kind before."

"Drool, did he just say drool? Well I've never drooled in my life. Who does he think he is?" Cleopatra was incensed. *"Estupido, where are you?"*

"Hey Cleo, I'm down here on the floor under you. Sorry I didn't respond faster, I think I have water in my ear from your drool."

Cleo hissed and jumped out of Peter's arms. *"Estupido, you better run for your life."*

***

Sheri took another look at Peter Arnstrom as he put Cleopatra down. "Hey, I know you. I mean, I know who you are. You were the star goalie of the Vancouver Canucks. Didn't you retire a couple years ago?"

Peter stood up and smiled. "You have a good memory. Yeah, that's me and yes, I'm retired. My family lives in Seattle and my dad needed me."

"You left a stellar career to live in a town without an NHL league? Actually, that's my favorite thing about Seattle, no NHL but it must kill you not to have a team here."

Sheri was thinking about Ice and wondering if Peter knew him.

"I'm an optimist; someday we'll have a team."

The reporter in Sheri took over. "Wait a minute; you grew up in Seattle with no team. How'd you get interested in the sport? How'd you turn pro?"

"You ask a lot of questions Miss McLellon, but I guess that's what you reporters do. See, I know a little about you too. Us ice jocks can read you know, and I never miss your column."

Sheri blushed with pleasure. "Thanks. But you didn't answer my question."

Peter picked up his toolbox. "I'll tell you what. You can shadow me while I work and I'll tell you the story as long as you don't print any of it. I like to maintain a low profile."

Walking to the back door, Peter set up his equipment. "When I was about fifteen, I started hanging out with a bad crowd. I was headed down the wrong path as my mom and dad kept telling me. My parents tried everything to straighten me out, but I wasn't buying what they were selling. Finally, in desperation, they shipped me over to Örnsköldsvik, Sweden to live with my mom's sister Ia and her family.

Long story short, my cousin, Jörgen, was totally into hockey. I started playing because there wasn't much else to do. Turns out, this little town in northern Sweden has produced quite a few NHL Hockey players. Players like Peter Forsberg, Markus Naslund, Niklas Sundstrom, Daniel and Henrik Sedin to name a few. The list is pretty long. Anyway, I started playing, and got hooked. I ended up begging my parents to let me stay for another year after my "sentence" was up. Örnsköldsvik gets a lot of NHL scouts coming to look at the players. I got drafted for the Canucks and that's pretty much it."

Sheri did a double take. "Wait, a modest hockey player. That's as common as a unicorn or a Mormon that doesn't tithe. Most of the ice jocks I know have had one too many pucks to the head and are show boaters."

"Hey, there are a lot of great guys in the league. They're not all crazy jocks looking to get their names in the headlines. And the news media doesn't help, always looking to exploit the bad stuff and ignoring the good things jocks do. As an example, hockey players do a lot of charity work for kid's causes and are just regular people. My buddy, Ice Zamboni, is the most generous guy I know. He's got a whole charity dedicated to kids and there are plenty more like him." Peter was starting to get a little pissed. Nobody dissed hockey players.

Sheri's jaw dropped. "You're friends with Ice Zamboni?"

"He's the president of the Minnesota NHL Alumni Association. That's the group of players that run a foundation to give money back to the community. There are other hockey charitable organizations that help children or battered women." Peter gave her a puzzled look while trying to figure out what her problem was with hockey players.

"I haven't seen him in years. We grew up together." Sheri wanted to end this conversation.

"Whoa, wait a minute. You're *that* Sheri? Oh man, I can see why you hate hockey players." Peter finally fit the last puzzle piece together.

"What do you mean, '*That* Sheri?' What has Ice said?" It was Sheri's turn to get angry.

"Ice and I were roommates for the entire season he was with the Canucks. We talked a lot. At the time, I was having problems with my girlfriend and Ice gave me some good advice."

"What possible advice could a womanizer like Ice give you on relationships?" Sheri spat out the words.

"He said, and I quote, 'Don't let the right one get away.' He told me that he had really screwed up and figured it out too late. He mentioned you many times."

Sheri was about to make a rude remark when her cell phone started ringing. She was relieved to have an excuse to end the conversation with Peter. He'd given her too much to think about.

Chapter 7

Trevor listened to Sheri's cell phone ringing. He was trying to figure out what kind of message to leave when he heard her voice snap, "This is Sheri McLellon."

"Hello Sheri, this is Trevor. I'm really sorry to bother you, but I was worried about you. Is everything okay at your house?"

Sheri let out the breath she'd been holding. For some reason, just talking about Ice had set her on edge. And for a moment she thought he'd be on the other end of the phone, conjured up by her conversation with Peter Arnstrom. "Everything is fine. The police were here and just as a precaution, I'm having my locks changed as we speak."

Trevor tried to remain calm. "Sounds like you're busy, I won't keep you. I just wanted to make sure you're ok. I'm looking forward to our dinner date tomorrow night."

"Me too, Trevor. I'll see you tomorrow. Bye."

Trevor disconnected the call and felt like throwing his phone against the wall. "Son-of-a-bitch. She's having the locks changed right now. This sucks. First the bug is ruined, and now the key is useless. Dammit."

Roger walked in rubbing ointment on his face. "Doesn't matter dude, I'm not going back into that house as long as the she-devil is still there. These scratches better not get infected. Man, I look like I've gone ten rounds with a cougar and I don't mean the hot older ones in bars."

"Quit being such a baby. You've screwed up every part of this job." Trevor grabbed a piece of beef jerky off the coffee table loaded with man food and sunk his teeth into a piece. "Thit Thit Thit."

"Dude, calm down. We'll figure this out."

"No you moron, my cap just fell off." Trevor ran into the bathroom and looked at his teeth. There was a gaping hole in his smile.

Roger was laughing like a hyena. "Oh my God, here it is the beginning of October and you look just like a jack-o'-lantern. Not a good look on you."

"Thut the fuck up you athhole. Do you know how much I paid for theeth teeth?"

"Trevor, if I was you, I'd worry more about your new lisp. Makes you sound like you were someone's bitch in prison."

"You athhole. How am I going to get thith fixed before my date with Theri?"

"If you can't get it fixed, just wear orange and black. Maybe she'll think it's a Halloween costume. Karma's a bitch, dude." Roger laughed and laughed, feeling better than he'd felt all day.

Trevor pulled out his cell phone and searched for emergency dental care. "There'th a place downtown, even advertises payment plans. Man, until my thip named Theri comes in, I've got to live on plastic. I hate being poor."

"Listen Trevor, if you don't figure this Sheri thing out and get the money, the way you look now, you'll be in a trailer park conning old ladies out of their social security checks. You won't even have to get your teeth fixed." Roger loved kicking Trevor when he was down.

"Yeah Roger, at least I can get my tooth fixed and look good. With those thcratches all over your thhaved head, it looks like you were trying on a live raccoon toupee."

Both men laughed and high-fived each other.

Chapter 8

Ice was trying to figure out how to communicate with Peter Arnstrom. *"Hey Buddy, it's me, Ice. Come on, take a good look. There must be some part of me in this little rat dog body."* Ice danced around Peter's feet. Finally, in desperation, he went into Sheri's home office and brought out the picture of him and Sheri.

"What do you have their little guy?" Peter reached down and took the picture frame from Ice's mouth. "Hey, I'd know this mug anywhere. That's Ice Zamboni. Why did you bring it to me?"

Peter looked from the picture down to the dog at his feet. Ice had been one of his best friends in the NHL. Too much time had passed since he'd talked to him. Peter always loved hanging out with Ice; there was never a dull moment. Ice was always the bright spot in the room and, like moths to a flame, the women flocked around him. Peter enjoyed being part of the inner circle and managed to do just fine with the ladies, too.

Something about hockey players and scars made women think they were bad boys, and Ice loved living up to the hype. Peter chuckled to himself. They were all blowing off steam in a local fishing hole. Ice was bored and pulled off his shirt to jump in for a swim. One of the not-so-bright models noticed a large birthmark on his back. "Ohh, look, Ice has a figure eight on his back. Is that a tattoo?" Peter remembered having a little fun with her. "Yeah, all of us players have hockey drills tattooed on our backs. Ice has the figure eight shooting and deflecting drill. During practice we play with our shirts off and the coach picks one of us to lead the team to do the drill on our back. Mine is called the 'Cycle give and Go.'"

The blonde model shivered, "My, you boys must get cold with your shirts off playing on the ice."

Peter remembered telling her, "Naw, we're tough and each player has a personal warmer in between drills. Maybe you'd like to try out? Come here, I'll show you what's needed."

Peter smiled at the memory. When he glanced

down at the little yapping dog, he jumped when he saw a perfect tan figure eight on the Chihuahua's back. "Holy shit, this is weird."

Ice sat in front of Peter and gave him a soulful look. His eyes were pleading for Peter to recognize him. That was when Peter noticed a scar over the little dogs left eye. Just like the scar Sheri gave Ice when she caught him with a fishhook.

Peter turned back to the lock on the door. He needed to finish this job and get out of here to think. Peter was as logical as the next person, as long as they, too, were raised by a mother who was a Swedish häxa and communicated with animals.

***

Sheri got off the phone from Trevor and walked back to the kitchen to see how the progress on the back door was going. "What's that picture doing out?"

Ice had the decency to look guilty and Peter just shrugged his shoulders. "Dog brought it out."

Sheri looked at Pablo, "Bad dog. What are you doing?"

Ice tucked his tail between his legs and assumed

the submissive position, one he was not used to.

Peter watched the interaction. If he believed in the nonsense his mother talked about, the fact that the figure eight was on the dog's back and the scar over his eye meant Pablo is Ice. In all the years Peter had known Ice, he never saw him act submissive. "I think your little dog just wanted to play. So this is you and Ice as kids?"

Sheri frowned and looked at Peter. "Look, I know you were friends with him, and so was I, a long time ago. Let's just get the locks changed so I can sleep peacefully tonight and, hopefully, tomorrow will be a better day."

"So you're the one that gave him the scar above his left eye?" Peter remembered comparing hockey scars with Ice. All players have remnants of hockey life displayed on their face. Ice had been proud of the fact he actually had a scar that wasn't from hockey. In fact, Peter remembered the story. "He got the scar when you two were fishing. Was it the day of this photo? Ice told me you tried to practice your casting and almost blinded him."

Peter was relieved when Sheri started to laugh.

"Oh, of course he would say that. Truth is, I was really good at casting. We used to practice and I always beat him. The day he got the scar is when he interfered just as I whipped the pole back and the hook got him. If he had just left it alone, nothing would have happened. Typical Ice in a nutshell. He didn't mind that I always got better grades than him but couldn't bear to let me excel in a sport."

"Sounds like you two were close."

"Yeah, for a long time we were, and then, we weren't. So how's the lock changing going?"

Peter could tell when a subject was over. "Fine, almost through. You know, Ice is the one who inspired me to give back to the community. He gave me the idea to start a hockey club for at-risk kids since, technically, I was one. You should come some time. We have games every Saturday. And next Friday night we have a big fundraiser auction. These kids can't afford to buy their equipment and my non-profit helps them out. It's a fun evening, great auction items, free booze and a pretty good dinner. I'd love to have you sit at my table. You can bring a friend if you'd like."

"Actually, I'd love to come. I always try to support kids' projects. Two questions: can I write about it in my column and can I bring my friend Johnni Wilson?"

Peter hadn't been living under a rock. "You mean *the* Johnni Wilson, Seattle's favorite daughter, top hot model, and brilliant marine biologist?"

"Wow, you must read all the fashion magazines. Do your hockey buddies know about your feminine side?"

Peter tilted his head and gave her an appraising look. "Jeez lady, you fight dirty. You must have picked it up from Ice. No, I don't read all the girly fashion magazines. Seattle natives all keep track of the local stars. Not to be immodest, but if you asked Johnni if she's heard about me, she'd say yes, even though we've never met."

Sheri was in a mood. "OK Lock Boy. Let's test your vain little comment. I'm texting Johnni right now." Picking up her phone, Sheri typed: Where are you, what are you doing? When did Trevor leave and have you ever heard of some guy named Peter Arnstrom?

Within seconds her phone buzzed. OMG, why did

you ask me about Peter Arnstrom? He's famous. Do you know him? Wait, you hate hockey guys. WTF?

Sheri smiled. "Oh, dang, guess you're right. She has heard of you. OK, I'm game. We'll come to your little soiree on Friday. Can you email me the details?"

Peter looked at the crazy redhead and remembered how Ice had expressed regret over losing her friendship and the possibility of anything else. "No problem, write your email address on my card. I'll send you all the info. And, yes, you can write about it. The publicity will be good for my kids." As Sheri turned to find a pen, Peter slipped the picture of her and Ice into his tool chest. He saw the dog wagging his tail. Peter looked at the figure eight on the little dog's back and the scar above his eye again and felt another shiver. *Damn, I'm turning into my mother. Something's going on here. Maybe mom can help me figure it out.*

When the three doors were finally rekeyed, Peter packed up his tools and was ready to leave. As he presented the bill to Sheri, he took a moment to look around. The living room was perfect blend of northwest casual and contemporary decor. The room was perfect, nothing out of place. A multi-colored throw was folded over the back of the beige leather sofa and he could see two books he knew were on the bestseller list sitting on end table next to a comfy looking one-piece recliner. The room was warm and inviting. The stone fireplace in the center of the room screamed for a cool fall night and a fire. Peter could imagine Sheri sitting in her recliner reading with a crackling fire. Peter thought of his friend Ice and decided a call was in order.

Sheri handed Peter her card with her email address. "Here's my home email. I'll look forward to coming to your fundraiser. And I'm sure you'll enjoy meeting Johnni."

Peter felt it would be to his benefit not to warn her that she and Johnni would be the only women at a table full of hockey jocks. He'd had two cancellations and smiled as he thought of sitting with the two unsuspecting women. Peter decided to not mention the girlfriend he'd referenced was long gone. Simone had traded him in for a football player. It still galled him to be dumped for an NFL quarterback.

***

Ice was watching Sheri get ready for bed. The little black dress had come off and he had a few brief minutes of watching her in her bra and thong while she brushed her teeth and washed her face. When the evening ritual ended with her putting on flannel pajamas and crawling into bed, Ice took that opportunity to jump on the bed and nestle in close to her head on the pillow. He breathed in her fragrance and gave a sigh of contentment. It was like the years between them had never happened and he felt peaceful for the first time in a long while. He lay there listening to her soft snores and wondering what would have happened if he'd taken her to the senior prom.

His peace was disrupted when he felt a large presence looming over his head. Looking up, he spotted Cleopatra with a scowl on her face. Not able to resist, he did something that resembled a dog smile, with his teeth showing. *"Hey Cleo baby, am I in your spot?"*

"Estupido, you have ten seconds to clear out of there or you'll be very, very sorry."

Ice was in such a good mood being this close to

Sheri he decided to be nice. *"Cleo, come snuggle next to me. We can share her and, with you close, I'll know she's protected."*

"Hmmppttt, well I guess that would be okay. At least you realize I'm more capable than you are of protecting her." Cleo lay down next to Ice but misjudged the space and half of her ended up on his head. *"Oh, sorry Estupido. You're so tiny, I didn't realize I was over too far."*

Ice thought to himself, *give 'em an inch and they'll take a mile. Last time I try sugar with this one. "No problem Cleo, you have so much girth it's probably hard to see your ass."*

Drifting off to sleep, Cleo could only manage to mumble, *"Estupido, I'll bite you tomorrow."*

Chapter 9

Warren Trimble was a man with a plan and his plan included Sheri. From the moment he first saw her, he knew she was the one. Now he just needed her to recognize the fact, too. Carefully combing his hair and splashing on just the right amount of cologne, he took a final look in the mirror and evaluated his image. He liked looking good. His grey Calvin Klein shirt and black pants were stylish but not too formal. Sperry Top-Sider shoes completed his ensemble. He thought, *I look like quite the catch if I do say so. My clothes say understated and approachable, not like that bozo Long and his pee-soaked Gucci loafers. He certainly can't be considered competition.*

Grabbing his keys, he headed out to his aging BMW. It was ten years old, but he kept it in tip-top shape. He bought it from a guy that moved up from Phoenix. The window tint was dark, especially for dreary Seattle days, but it sometimes came in handy when people couldn't see in the car.

It was a sunny October day. Cool weather in the high 50's and a clear blue sky. It was cold enough for sweaters or a light jacket but warm enough to remind you that summer was barely over. Warren threw a jacket in his back seat and verified his stun gun, handcuffs and duct-tape were stashed under the driver's seat.

Driving down Market Street to the restaurant, Warren noticed women walking along the sidewalk and thought none of them compared to the natural beauty of Sheri McLellon. There was something captivating about her. Reading her articles in the newspaper and watching her from afar the past six months had Warren excited to finally spend time with Sheri in person. In his best Bogart voice, "this could be the start of a beautiful relationship." Warren was determined it would be.

Finding a parking spot by Maximilian's, Warren took a second to survey his surroundings, noting what cars were around him and if any were occupied. As he approached the restaurant, he noted the emergency side door on the south side of the restaurant. Always good to know.

A smiling hostess greeted him as he opened the front door. Warren looked at her and smiled. "I'm meeting a young lady for lunch; can we get a table by the window?"

"Yes sir. We don't have many tables occupied right now. You're just before the noon rush, you can have your pick."

Warren was led to the window tables and chose one that would give his lunch partner a view of the water while he had a view of the entire restaurant. "The young lady is named Sheri. I'm sure she'll be here soon."

He hadn't been seated but a couple of minutes when he saw Sheri walking towards him. Warren watched her every move, appreciating her grace and the fluidity of her movements. She looked both athletic and feminine, a delightful combination. X-rated thoughts started going through Warren's mind and he did his best to quell them as she stood in front of him. Rising, he wasn't sure if he should shake her hand or do a Hollywood air kiss. He decided to just stand with a goofy grin on his face. "Sheri, I'm so glad you're here."

Sheri slid into the chair. She noticed how

handsome Warren appeared and how his grey shirt set off his blue grey eyes.

The waitress handed them menus and took their drink orders.

When she left, Warren was the first one to break the ice. "Sheri, I have to tell you that I know a little bit about you. I read your column every day. You really have a way of making the reader feel like they were right at the game. Plus, some of the in-depth interviews you've done have really been enlightening on the personalities of our pro sports players."

"Well, since you know so much about me, let's talk about you. Are you a Seattle native?"

Warren laughed, "Does the mold around my ears and the webbed fingers give me away? Yes, born and raised here. I went to high school in Ballard and college at the UW."

"You sure didn't wander too far did you?"

"Actually, I did. After the service I spent four years wandering around the country, trying to find a place more beautiful than Seattle. When I realized I couldn't, I came home." Warren's mind was playing pictures of the various places he had lived. "What about you? I know you're originally from Minnesota. What brought you out here?"

Sheri reached out for a piece of bread. "I came out here for college. Looks like we're both Dawgs. I was intent on becoming a nuclear physicist."

Warren had his margarita coming out his nose. "A nuclear physicist? You're kidding right?" Grabbing a napkin, he tried to get the drink off his face.

"Wait a minute, why are you so shocked at that? I had a 4.0 GPA, was on the Dean's list and really excelled in math and science." Sheri was a little insulted.

Warren realized his mistake. "I'm sorry, you're just so beautiful. I know you have beauty and brains, I just kind of thought nuclear physicist sounded pretty dry and boring." Trying to dig himself out of the hole he had dug, he said, "OK, so what happened?"

"I was writing a sports column for the campus newspaper and I had quite a following. I used to be kind of a tomboy and played a lot of sports. Plus, my best friend growing up was a guy, and we argued sports statistics a lot. It became second nature for me to scan all the stats everyday."

At the mention of best friend, Ice perked up and let out a little woof.

"Hush Pablo. Sorry Warren, I had to bring him. I'm not totally convinced that my cat won't eat him if I leave the two of them alone."

Warren looked at the end of her purse and could see two little eyes staring back at him. "Hey buddy, remember me?"

They could hear a thumping of his tale against the purse.

"Sounds like he does. Anyway, I was getting bored being a research assistant and spending all my time alone in a lab. I guess the passion just wasn't there. When I got an offer from the largest newspaper in the state, I jumped at it. All in all, it's been great. I love sports and its fun getting ringside seats to Mariners and Seahawks games. Too bad those are our only two major league sports, but it's ok for now."

Warren was kind of a sports buff but decided not to take her on. "So, you usually have to work all the big games? Do you ever get to watch sports for fun? I play hockey for a neighborhood league. We play once a week."

The color drained out of Sheri's face. Really? The guy seemed perfect but he was just another ice jock wannabe? "Gee, I don't think so. I pretty much got my fill of hockey at home in Minnesota. But thanks."

Warren was kicking himself. He remembered her comments at the lake the day her purse got taken. She called hockey players dumb ice jocks. Darn. Now what?

"It was just a suggestion. I also have a lot of other interests. Movies, books, Bingo. Ok, I'm lying about Bingo, unless you're interested in it then I will be. Come on, give me some help here. I'm dying!"

Sheri laughed. "Sorry, I just have bad hockey memories. Kind of a post-traumatic stress thing. I start thinking about freezing my butt off, bad cocoa, and pucks going crazy. Not a great time in my life. I like movies and books. I bet you go for the books where the bad guy is always busted by the overworked, underpaid cop."

Warren gave her a funny look. "No, actually I like the psychological thrillers where the villain is always one step ahead of the cops. Makes it more interesting."

**

Hearing those words and the odd tone to his voice, Ice gave an involuntary shiver thinking, *something's not quite right with Detective Perfect.*

As Ice sat in Sheri's dog purse, he listened to the banter between the two and thought about what to do. The biggest threat was the creepy Trevor and the Ass Man. Detective Perfect would be good to keep around until Ice could sort things out.

**

Sheri didn't know when she had laughed so hard. She couldn't decide if Warren was really funny, or if the margaritas were too strong. She realized Warren was an expert at getting people to talk about themselves and she still knew very little about him. "Warren, are you ready for our walk. I hear Pablo starting to stir in my purse. Must be potty time."

Warren peeked into her purse. "I can't believe he just sits there so quietly. Ok buddy, let's get you outside."

Walking out of the restaurant, Warren noticed

other diners watching Sheri. Thinking to himself, *she always lights up a room. It's the first thing I noticed about her. And the beautiful red hair. I bet she has a fiery temper to go with it. She's going to be a challenge.*

***

Sheri pulled Ice out of her purse and snapped a leash on him. He stopped for a moment and took it all in. Waves were gently lapping against the shore, and the sandy beach made him itch to run. A majestic mountain range framed the picture. Ice realized this was one of the reasons Sheri loved living in Seattle. She had always been into nature and hiking when they were kids. He turned to Sheri and put his front paws on her leg. Wagging his tail and raising his lips, he looked up and gave her his best dog grin.

"Oh my God. Look, Pablo is smiling! I've only seen a couple dogs in my life do that. Pablo, are you a happy boy? Look at my happy boy!"

Warren watched the interaction and hid his irritation at being upstaged by a dog.

He looked at Sheri's obvious pleasure in the little dog and jealousy gnawed at him. "So the dog wasn't chipped? Did you try the lost and found or Craigslist? Someone must be looking for this little guy. He's such a charmer."

"I have to confess, I haven't done anything past verifying if he was chipped. I'll check the ads when I get home. Someone must be missing him. He's pretty darn cute and smart, too." Sheri reached down and unclipped the dog leash to give Pablo a chance to run around a bit.

The dog took off at a dead run heading towards the water. He played chicken with the waves and then ran large circles around Sheri and Warren until he finally flopped down in the sand, exhausted and panting. *What is it about dogs and running around in circles? It's like I'm possessed. I must be about fifty in dog years and I'm feeling every one of them. Jeesh!*

"Looks like your little dog is worn out." Warren was happy. Maybe now the dog would sleep while he and Sheri took their walk.

"Oh Pablo, you do look beat. Come here, we'll put you back in the purse."

Ice started walking towards Sheri, then on impulse

he walked over to Warren and gave him a good sniff. Sheri squatted down with the leash in her hand and Ice wagged his tail and licked her face thinking, *I'm going to protect you no matter what size I am. I've missed you so much.*

Sheri squealed as he licked her face. "Ok Pablo, I get it. You love me. Let's get you back in the purse so you can nap."

Ice complied and as he went into the bag he took one last look at his competition. Warren stood by with a pleasant look on his face but there was something in his eyes that made Ice wonder.

***

Sheri let herself into her house and called for Cleopatra as she tapped her code into the alarm system. Ice squirmed his way out of her purse and ran into the bedroom looking for Cleo.

"Hey bad ass cat, where are you?"

"Estupido, how's the purse puppy? Did you have fun eavesdropping on Sheri's date all day?"

"It was pretty boring. Something about that guy, Warren. I can't put my finger on, or, I should say my paw on, but he's weird. Not as weird as Trevor, the guy she's going out with

tonight."

"I hate that you're getting all the action and I'm stuck here. It's not fair."

Ice was nothing if not a good manipulator of females. *"But Cleo, you're the one that's guarding the house. Just think what would have happened if you hadn't been here when the guy got in last night. You saved the day."*

Cleo started purring, *"Yes and I'm so exhausted. I had to stay up all night guarding the house while you were licking Sheri's shoulder as she slept. You are so disgusting."*

Ice had the good grace to look embarrassed. *"I can't help it. She's so beautiful and I've missed her so much. I just kind of snuggled close and when I sniffed her I couldn't resist a few licks."*

"Yeah Estupido, you're going to get real far with her in that body."

"Remember, once we save her, I won't be in this body. I'm coming back as me as soon as I can."

Cleo looked at Ice. *"I know you will and maybe, just maybe, I won't mind you being here, as long as Sheri's happy."*

Chapter 10

Trevor was in pain. His front tooth was fixed with a temporary cap and the pain pills were making him woozy. He had exactly four hours to get his act together before meeting Sheri at the Jade Palace. He opened the door to his apartment and made it as far as the sofa before passing out. Even with the pain pills, he felt like his teeth were on fire and firemen with size fourteen boots were trying to stomp it out. He didn't know how he was going to get through his date. Being a charming dinner date did not sound like something he could pull off tonight and charm was all he had to go on. He'd always been the pretty boy, not the smart boy. In fact, he wouldn't have made it out of high school if he hadn't slept with Miss Miller, the guidance counselor. She had been an unmarried thirty-two year old, and what she lacked in looks, she made up for in her ability to change his grades. It took a little persuasive blackmail but was worth it. The day he graduated high school, he left a smarter, wiser guidance counselor behind. Miss Miller was thankful she hadn't been caught and henceforth, curbed her propensity for sleeping with male students.

Trevor crashed hard for three hours and when he woke up, Roger was standing over him. "Dude, wake up. You're meeting her in an hour."

"How does this tooth look? It's a temporary but it looks okay, right?"

Roger took a look and tried to keep his face neutral. "Sure, looks fine. It's a dark restaurant right? Maybe she won't notice the color difference."

Trevor shrieked like a girl. "Color difference, are you kidding me?" He jumped off the sofa and ran into the bathroom. Looking at himself in the mirror he tried to convince himself that the cut-rate dentist hadn't blown it. "I guess you get what you pay for. The temporary looks off."

***

An hour later Trevor was pulling into a parking spot at the Jade Palace. His head was still a little woozy from the pain pills and he was trying to walk straight and not stumble as he pushed the door to the restaurant open. The light was dim and he said a silent prayer of thanks to the god of bad intentions, sure that his tooth problem would not be evident. While he was waiting for the hostess, Sheri walked in the door.

Trevor pasted on a lopsided grin, no teeth showing. He had to admit, she was a good looking woman. Not quite his type but it could have been worse. Even if she had weighed 500 pounds with a face that could curdle cream, he still would have put his plan into action.

Turning on the charm, Trevor took her hand and said, "I've been looking forward to this evening."

Sheri smiled and withdrew her hand, noticing his was a bit clammy and damp. "Me too. We haven't really had a chance to chat."

As they were being led to their table, Trevor was walking behind Sheri and looking around the room to make sure he didn't run into anyone that knew him. He was relieved to see that their table was in a back corner with only a flickering candle for lighting. He was sure the hostess thought this was a romantic dinner because she winked at him as she walked away.

Trevor's plan was to ask Sheri all about her life in hopes of gleaning some of the information he needed to do an identity theft. However, it was soon evident that Sheri was the one conducting an interview.

"So Trevor, you know what I do for a living, but I don't know a thing about you. What do you do?"

Trevor decided to stick with as close to the truth as possible. "Well, up until last year I was employed at a land development company as the Accounts Payable Manager. My talents were wasted there. I basically took their money and invested it in several revenue-producing ventures, mainly pharmaceuticals and the travel industry. The results were better than the company expected and they wanted to promote me to Chief Financial Officer but I declined and actually left the company. I spent the next year locked away, working on my own investments. I was fortunate that some influential people took notice and now I have three clients for which I handle their investments. I would tell you their names but then I'd have to kill you. They value their privacy."

Trevor's little joke fell flat and he scrambled to recover.

Sheri looked at him, "It's ok, I took a picture of your license plate just in case."

Trevor panicked thinking his goose was cooked when he realized, she had no idea what car he drove. "Aren't you the funny one! You had me going for a moment. All I could think of was I should have washed my car before you saw it."

Sheri laughed but had seen his absolute look of panic and wondered what that was all about.

The rest of the evening went well. Trevor talked about himself incessantly but Sheri chalked it up to nerves. When the last of the dessert dishes had been cleared away, the waiter brought their bill, laying it in front of Trevor. Sheri reached over and grabbed the bill. "Please, this is my treat. You ran after a mugger and got my purse back. I can't thank you enough."

Trevor was relieved. He was starting to sweat knowing the credit card he was using was maxed out after the trip to the dentist. "I'm glad I could help a lady in distress. I'd love to see you again."

Sheri thought back to Johnni's words and inwardly sighed. Figuring one more date wouldn't kill her, she replied "Sure, that would be lovely. You have my number."

Trevor walked Sheri to her car and when he leaned in to try and kiss her, she put the car door between them. "Well, good night." Sheri got into her car and used her blue-tooth to call Johnni.

Johnni picked up on the first ring. "You're calling early, must have been a bad date."

"The worst date ever. The guy talked about himself all night long."

"Sheri, he was just trying to impress you. Give the guy a break."

There was a long silence on the other end of the phone before Sheri finally spoke. "There's something odd about this guy. He kept dropping hints about money and if I needed someone to invest for me. I have a weird feeling about him."

Johnni made a strangled noise. "I wasn't going to say anything but he was very evasive when I interrogated, I mean, tried to chat with him at the bar the other night."

Sheri snorted. "You were right the first time; I think interrogated is probably more fitting. You know, I'm going to check out our Mr. Trevor Long. Something doesn't add up. I've had too many weird coincidences since I've met him. Purse snatched, possible break in, a bug on my phone and Pablo hates him. That's got to mean something, too."

"You're not kidding. Your little dog had some mighty big growls when that guy was around. I thought your puppy purse was going to explode and a frothing super dog hero pit bull was going to jump out." Johnni took a sip of her chardonnay.

Sheri stopped at a red light. "You know, I've got an account through work that gives me access to people's credit scores, work and criminal history. I'll do a search on our little Trevor Long and see what game he's playing. Something is up. You're spending the night when we go to the Gala so we can work on it the next day."

Johnni thanked God that Sheri was on her side. The girl was genius when it came to ferreting out information on people. "Sounds good. Whatever you find, can I watch when you sic Pablo on him?"

Sheri laughed. "You betcha! I have a feeling this is about my uncle's money. We'll talk more later. See you tomorrow."

Sheri disconnected the call and a light bulb went off in her head. For months, she had been begging her boss to give her an assignment with some teeth to it. Writing about athletes was getting a little too routine. She needed to do some investigative writing and now she had her chance. Sheri had been reading about internet scams, serial killers and Ponzi schemes for years. She wanted to get in on the action.

Chapter 11

The next day Johnni rang Sheri's doorbell and then opened the front door. "Girl, this door should be locked. What are you thinking?"

"I'm thinking that my best friend is on her way and wouldn't have enough patience for me to walk from the bedroom to the front door before barging in. Wow, you look amazing. The dress is stunning and fits you like it was made for you."

"Actually, this dress is one that will be in Cosmopolitan Magazine next month. Sometimes I barter and lower my rate to get a dress or two. Speaking of that, check out what I brought for you to wear."

Sheri hadn't noticed the garment bag in Johnni's hand. "Still don't trust me to pull off dressing myself do you?" Sheri laughed as she grabbed the bag and unzipped the long zipper. "Oh my, this is heavenly. Johnni, I can't wear this, it must have cost a fortune!"

"You are going to look amazing in this dress and don't worry about anything else. This is a Cinderella loan for the night. We're the same size and even though I'm three inches taller, it will still work. Besides, that will bring the length down to your nun standards!"

"Oh stop, I'm not that bad! Sheri slipped off her robe and put the shimmery dress on. It was emerald green and fit her perfectly. The scooped neckline showed off a hint of cleavage and the stretchy material made her backside rival JLo's. "I think I have some jewelry that will be perfect for this."

When Sheri returned from her bedroom, she had a costume jewelry necklace of rhinestones and green emeralds that set off her long neck. Dainty rhinestone and emerald earrings completed the look. Johnni had her turn around twice and watched how the dress hung on all her curves. A wide smile lit up her face. "Girl, you have always been beautiful, but tonight you are positively radiant! See what happens when you have a few men buzzing around you."

Sheri started to disagree and gave up. "Thank you. I love this dress. It fits perfectly and I actually feel like I'm starting a new chapter in my life. Let me get my shoes and we're ready to go." Going back to her closet, Sheri selected a pair of black stiletto heels that showed off her shapely legs. The shoes would kill her feet by the end of the evening but were worth the pain. Grabbing her evening purse and a black satin coat, her look was complete.

***

When Johnni and Sheri arrived at the Seattle Convention Center, they parked the car and headed to the elevator. Johnni looked over at Sheri, "Now tell me the scoop on Peter Arnstrom. Does he have a girlfriend? Is he as gorgeous as he looks on TV? Is he nice?"

"You have a lot of questions. Two of them you can answer yourself in a few minutes. The girlfriend thing I'm not sure about. Sounds like he does, but since he took relationship advice from Ice Zamboni, it's probably doubtful. We'll find out soon enough."

Checking in the two women were given packets with their bidding numbers and table assignment. Sheri was not surprised to see their table was number one.

Right up front for all the live auction action. Wandering around the room, they were thrilled to see the merchandise on the silent auction tables. After accepting a glass of wine from a passing waiter, the girls settled in to some serious shopping. Sheri wanted to make sure she lent some support to this charity. Having done some research on Peter's charity, she decided that an anonymous donation would be coming their way. Sheri had just completed the paperwork to turn her uncles' money into a charitable trust, thinking it would be in keeping with his final wishes. It still bothered her that she hadn't gotten to know him better before he passed away. And it mystified her that he had selected her to leave his fortune to. At any rate, this was her first venture into being a benefactress.

She was startled to feel a hand on her back as she leaned over to bid on an auction item. Turning, she saw Peter Arnstrom with a big smile on his face and a lovely woman on his arm. For a moment she thought Peter was dating a cougar, but when the woman smiled, she realized that grin could only come from a proud mother.

"Peter, you startled me. This is lovely, you must

be so happy how the evening is going."

Peter Arnstrom did a quick once-over, taking in the way her dress hugged her in all the right places and the color set off her beautiful green eyes. Even though he didn't quite have all the pieces to the puzzle, he knew he would never make a move on Sheri until he figured out what was going on with Ice, who he planned on calling after the event. "Talk about looking incredible, you look beautiful. Speaking of beautiful let me introduce you to my mother, Britt Louise."

Sheri looked into blue eyes that were identical to Peter's. "It's a pleasure to meet you Mrs. Arnstrom. You must be very proud."

Britt Louise smiled and grasped Sheri's hand. "Please, call me Britt Louise. It is a pleasure to meet you. My husband reads your column every day and likes to share some of the articles with me. You have an astute way of reporting facts. We enjoy it very much."

Sheri blushed with pleasure. "Thank you for the lovely compliment. I hear a very slight accent. Your son says you're from Sweden?"

"Yes. When I was eighteen, I came to America to

attend college. I meet Peter's father and three years later we were married. I love the United States but I miss Sweden and do frequent trips back to see my family."

As his mother was talking, Peter's eyes widened as he looked beyond Sheri's shoulder. In an awestruck voice that almost sounded like a boy going through puberty, he did a strangled whisper, "It's her. Oh my God, you really brought Johnni Wilson. She's so beautiful."

As Peter's eyes were bugging out of his head, Johnni walked up to the group. "Hello, I'm Johnni. It's a pleasure to finally meet you Peter."

Fair skinned blondes have a hard time hiding a blush, and Peter was no exception. He was so star-struck he was momentarily at a loss for words. Peter's mother stepped in. "Hello Johnni. I'm Peter's mother, Britt Louise. I think my son is a little tongue-tied right now. Welcome to the auction. We're delighted you could join us this evening."

Johnni laughed and shook the beautiful older woman's hand. "He's not the only star-struck person around here." Looking at Peter she smiled and said, "I followed your career for years. I'm a huge fan."

Peter finally managed to speak, "OK, enough of the mutual admiration society meeting. I'm pleased to have two lovely ladies at my table this evening. Mom and dad have a group of friends at the table next to us."

Britt Louise looked at her son with a mock stern expression. "You make sure you and those other Neanderthals behave or I'll throw a dinner roll at you."

All three laughed and Peter had the good grace to tell his mother he would make sure that everyone behaved because he knew, from experience, that she would make good on her threat.

**

As soon as Sheri saw the other seven people seated at table number one, 'It's Raining Men' started playing in her head again. She couldn't stop it. All seven of the men were obvious jocks, and even though she professed not to follow hockey, she knew their names, and her mind was quickly recalling stats.

Johnni let out a little squeal. "Girl, we have hit the mother lode here."

Sheri nudged her in the ribs. "Would you please

be quiet?"

Johnni nudged Sheri. "Looks like we have to share him tonight."

Peter had arranged the table so there was a seat available on either side of him. He stood when the ladies approached the table. "Hello ladies, how was your bidding?"

Johnni clapped her hands with glee. "Very successful! I bid on two paintings, the Oktoberfest bucket of German beers, some jewelry and a few other things. I hate to be greedy but I got them all!"

Sheri smoothed out her dress as she sat down. "Yes, it's so amazing when you skip right to the "get it now price", you usually win the bid. Lucky for you, my friend loves to support a good cause and hates standing around waiting to see if she won a bid."

"How about you Sheri? Did you find anything?"

"Let's just say that I wish my car was bigger. It's going to be a challenge to get this all home."

Immediately all the jocks started talking at once. Peter silenced them and with a huge smile said, "Ladies, we are all at your disposal. We'd be happy to help two magnanimous supporters for our charity. We'll carry everything out at the end of the evening."

"That sounds very nice. Peter, are you going to introduce us to your helpful friends?" Johnni smiled her mega-watt smile around the table, and Peter watched in amusement as he saw his friends turn into flustered fifteen year-old boys.

Peter was a charming host and Sheri watched with interest as he engaged Johnni in conversation and did his best to include his friends.

"Johnni, I remember reading that you majored in Marine Biology." Peter watched as all eyes turned on Johnni.

"Yes, I got my degree in Marine Biology. I got sidetracked when I started modeling to help pay for my tuition. I'm still very active in Marine Biology. My specialty is sharks. I usually spend at least two months a year on a boat somewhere in the world, tracking, analyzing and studying the sharks from a shark cage or just swimming with them."

Peter's eyes got wide. "Let me get this straight. You actually swim with sharks? And you go down in a shark cage? Wow Johnni, you've got a set on you."

Just as he said the words that were meant as a compliment, his mother happened to be walking by. "Peter Arnstrom! You leave the hockey talk on the ice or in the locker-room and not in front of these two charming ladies."

Peter had the decency to look contrite and Johnni gave a good natured laugh. "Britt Louise, I travel with men on a ship out at sea. Believe me, I've heard worse. And it was supposed to be a compliment."

Britt Louise glared at her son and said very quietly in Swedish, "Du är klädd som en gentleman, börja bete dig som en."

"Peter sighed and replied "Ja mamma."

Sheri watched the exchange and could tell that Peter had been scolded by his mother. She looked at him with a glint in her eyes. "What did your mother have to say?"

With a lopsided grin Peter replied. "If I'm going to dress like a gentleman I need to act like a gentleman."

Johnni heard the exchange and gave Peter a little nudge. "It's okay, I know you meant it as a compliment.

Actually I've been told that before. Some of the dives we go on are pretty intense."

Sheri leaned over. "If you think she's brave diving with sharks, you should see her on the mean streets of New York City. One time she went all ninja warrior on a mugger that tried to take her purse. The guy was so scary that I would rather have faced off sharks. But Johnni just knocked him to the ground with a strategic kick to his groin and stood on this throat until the cops came. She was all calm, cool and collected."

Peter couldn't help but put his hand to his throat while the other men at the table that overheard the story scrunched up a bit in their nether region. They all looked at her with a little fear and silently vowed to make sure they stayed on her good side.

In a falsetto voice Peter said, "I admire a woman that can take care of herself and I promise to never touch your purse if you promise not to go ninja on me!"

Everyone laughed and the talk soon turned to hockey war stories and fights on the ice. Sheri couldn't help but laugh and realized while she still vowed to never go to another hockey game, she missed watching it. She couldn't count the number of times she saw Ice right in the middle of all the action and, for a moment, missed him terribly.

Chapter 12

The next morning Sheri and Johnni were lingering over coffee after a scrumptious breakfast. Ice was sitting by Sheri looking up at her with adoring eyes as she absent-mindedly rubbed his belly. Finally Sheri pulled out a sheath of papers she had copied from her search on Trevor Long. "Johnni, this is too weird to be true. I checked out Trevor Long and I have great news!"

Johnni arched her eyebrow. "He's not a criminal or a homicidal maniac?"

"Oh no. He's a criminal all right. In fact, he just got out of minimum security prison. The man is obviously a total idiot but a handsome one. I checked his high school grades. He skated through sophomore, junior and the first three quarters of his senior year on D's or F's in most of his classes. Then, in the fourth quarter of his senior year, he got straight A's which brought up his sad GPA and made him eligible to graduate with his class. Hmm. Interesting. He didn't go to college, but it looks like from his social security review he worked a number of jobs until he landed with a land development company." Sheri continued to scan the documents. "Oh my God. He is really a piece of work. He just so happens to be the nephew of the lawyer my uncle used for his will. His uncle was his lawyer for his embezzlement charges. That explains how he latched onto me. I bet this whole thing is a set-up, starting with the purse snatching. He must be trying to figure out how to get his hands on my uncle's money!"

Johnni clenched her right hand into a fist. "That sorry- assed liar better make sure I don't see him first." As she spoke, Ice yipped in agreement and growled. Johnni looked over at Ice. "I told you that was a smart dog."

"No, don't you see. This is perfect. We know his game now. I can write a story about this and get him busted. I'm a little put out that he's trying to figure out how to transfer the money rather than sweep me off my feet and marry me. What a loser. What am I, chopped liver?" Sheri found it insulting as an intelligent woman and also as someone that had fought her insecurities about her looks. She still didn't believe the ugly duckling was now a swan. She really wanted to nail this guy.

"What's your plan?"

Sheri thought for a moment. "This will be like taking candy from a baby. I'm sure Trevor has no way of knowing all the money has been put into an endowment fund for various charities. I'm going to tell him I'm in need of a money manager. He'll bite. I can't believe he was stupid enough to use his real name."

***

Ice jumped off the sofa and ran to find Cleopatra. *"Hey bad- ass cat, wake up and get out here quick. They're talking about Trevor and ass man."*

Cleopatra opened her emerald green eyes and let out a delicate yawn. *"If you would do your fair share of guarding Sheri, I could sleep nights and most of the day like I'm supposed to. I was up all night, again!! So don't tell me to wake up now. I need my beauty sleep."*

Ice was getting cranky. *"Cleo, there is no arguing that*

you need your beauty sleep but this is important and I need your brains. Sheri and Johnni figured out Trevor is after the money but something isn't sitting well with me. This was too easy. Plus, Sheri is obviously able to take care of the problem. I don't think this is why I was sent here. Something else is going down."

"Estupido, you are being way too dramatic. What else could it be? I think you just don't want to leave her because she won't speak to you again once you're back to being human."

Ice growled, still dismayed at how wimpy it sounded. But he needed to let off some steam. *"Cleo, you get your furry, fat cat ass up off that bed and come into the living room right now. I'm serious, we need to be on the lookout for whatever the real problem is. This Trevor guy is like an annoying fly, but he's not smart enough to be dangerous."*

"Oh all right. Hold your teeny tiny horses. I'm right behind you."

Ice ran back to the living room, and as he started to reclaim his spot by Sheri, he heard Cleo. *"Don't even think about it Estupido. It's my turn."*

Realizing he needed Cleo, he gave in and went up to Johnni and whimpered.

"Oh sweet boy, do you want to sit on my lap?

Come on." Johnni leaned down and Ice was treated to a view of her cleavage and then placed on her lap as she stroked his ears and petted him. Ice was in heaven. He loved super models and his tail was thumping on her lap. *Who says it's a dog's life? This is heaven!*

Cleo looked over and watched Ice as she pretended not to enjoy Sheri's cuddling. Finally, unable to contain herself, she started purring, making a sound so loud it sounded like a drone was circling the living room.

"Aww Cleo, listen to you purr. That's my baby." Sheri cooed to her cat. "See Johnni, she pretends she doesn't like attention but she's a pushover."

Ice did his dog smile and Johnni looked down. "Damn, there it is again. This dog is smiling. Okay, so where were we?"

Sheri picked up the papers again. "When we were in school, remember our psychology class and the talk about criminal behavior and IQ's? If I remember correctly, most, but not all, serial killers have very high IQ's. That's why it's so hard to catch them. But, petty criminals like Trevor are usually below average. When I checked his high-school records I found that he was on the high end of the lower IQ spectrum. To me he looks like a guy that has gotten by on his looks and has exploited anyone he comes in contact with."

Johnni looked over at her friend. "So, what you're saying is he isn't smart enough to be a serial killer so we shouldn't worry about that?"

"No. Like I said, there are exceptions to every rule but I feel pretty strongly that he's not a violent criminal. I think he is after money and if he was smart or violent, he would have stormed the house and put a gun to my head to have the money transferred somewhere out of the country. I think he's like one of those guys on the internet that has women fall in love with him and he takes their money. Obviously, the man has no computer skills or he would have tried a different approach on this whole thing." Sheri spoke confidently and Ice was listening and pondering her words.

"So what's your plan? Are you going to do hidden cameras and recorders? Will I be at command central while all this is going down?" Johnni was starting to warm up to the idea of taking Trevor down.

"I'm not sure if we can be that high tech. I need to talk to my boss. The problem is, I don't want them to know about the money from my uncle."

"Sheri, you gave all the money away. It's not in your name. You made sure your only access to it was through the foundation and it has to go through the board members. By the way, thank you for asking me to be one."

"You're welcome. Yeah, you're right. I just didn't want anyone to start thinking it was *my* money and deciding I really didn't need a job anymore."

"Girl, you are trippin'. You know you're the most sought after sportswriter in the country. How many job offers have you turned down? There's no way they would ever lay you off."

"Okay Johnni, you're right. Wow, you played that 'voice of reason' card at the right moment. I think this whole thing has me a little on edge. I don't like being a target. It does make me laugh at how charming he's trying to be. I should have spotted him right away as a hustler. Who wears Gucci shoes to walk around Green Lake?"

At the mention of the Gucci shoes, Ice did another big dog smile.

Chapter 13

Trevor was whistling. He felt good about his date with Sheri last night, especially since she really did pick up the check. The type of women he was usually attracted to never paid for anything. He chuckled to himself thinking, *well, not in cash anyway. They always managed to barter something worth having. I sure won't be getting that from our little Miss McLellon. She looks like she has the four-date rule stamped on her ass. I should be long gone with her cash by date number three.*

A knock at the door startled him. Opening it up, he saw Roger standing there with a distressed look on his face. "What's up? You look like you just lost your last friend."

Roger slugged him in the arm as he walked into the apartment. "You are my last friend and probably one I should lose. I just tried to buy another bug for

Sheri's phone. No can do. I don't have enough cash and I know you don't. These people aren't the kind to take credit cards."

As they were pondering their next step, Trevor's cell phone rang. He smiled wide when he saw the caller ID. "Well, hello Sheri. Nice to hear from you."

"Trevor, I had such a good time the other night with you. It was fascinating to hear about your investments and how well you do. I know you said you weren't taking on anymore clients but I was wondering if you could give me some financial advice."

Sheri's voice was dripping with sincerity. Johnni was sitting in the chair silently making gagging noises.

"Well, thank you. I have been very successful investing other people's money. I'm really not looking to take on anymore clients. I like to give one on one attention to all my accounts so I keep the number of investors small." Trevor was enjoying himself and let a long pause go by while he let her sweat. "I really enjoy your company and would like to see more of you. So I guess, as long as it doesn't interfere with our personal relationship, I could add you to my client list."

"Oh, could you? I have had such a hard time finding someone I feel that would do a good job." Sheri was almost gagging at the words as she said them. "Maybe we could get together at your office to discuss this?"

Trevor started to panic. How the hell was he going to pull this off? All of a sudden inspiration hit. "I'm going to be at a conference for the next four days. I can drop by a form for you to fill out and we can start setting up the account. This will also give me a chance to find out what kind of investments you're looking for."

"Perfect." Sheri thought for a moment. She had no doubt he knew where she lived but still didn't want him at her house. "You're probably pretty busy today but if you want, we could meet for coffee and you could give me the forms."

"Sure. That works. Pick a Starbucks....there's one on almost every corner of Seattle."

Sheri did a girlish giggle and then inwardly gagged. "Trevor, you're so funny and you're in such a serious profession. Let's meet at the Starbucks on 85th and Greenwood Ave. Does 3:00 p m work for you?"

"It's a date. See you there." Trevor's arm shot into the air to high five Roger as he hung up the phone. "She wants to invest with my "firm." Now, where are those forms we copied? I'll have all of her personal information in a few hours and the rest, as they say, will be history. Those funds will be transferred soon!"

***

Sheri got off the phone and both she and Johnni started to laugh. Ice just stared at them. He looked over at Cleo. *"Why do females laugh at the dumbest things? This is not funny. I don't feel good about this at all. Even though we don't think the problem is Trevor, we still need to watch him. I'm going outside to do my business. That's when I do my best thinking."*

Cleo sniffed the air. *"Yes, by all means. If you do your best thinking crouched out in the back yard, go for it."*

Ice started the potty dance and Johnni scooped him up. "Looks like this little guy needs to go outside. I'll take him. You need to call your boss and figure things out. I can be your camera woman in the coffee shop but I'll need a good disguise."

"Okay, let me call Russ and then we'll figure out

how to dress you. I'm thinking maybe as a man." Sheri snickered when she saw the look of horror on Johnni's face.

***

The minute Ice was outside he started peeing on everything in sight. *"Damn. This is fun!"* Ice continued to run around the yard spreading his scent until he came to a screeching stop. He followed the scent all around the backyard until it stopped right under the window to Sheri's bedroom. *"I know this smell. What's it doing here?"* Ice ran back up to the back door and when Johnni opened it he shot straight to where Cleo was laying. *"Cleo, it's the cop. He's the danger."*

Chapter 14

Seattle was the eighth major city Jon Albert Culver had lived in and there was a murdered redhead in seven of them. He was convinced he was smarter than the cops and he would never be caught. Tonight was the night for number eight. He was rushing it with Sheri, but the itch was so strong, he couldn't wait to scratch it.

Jon Albert loved his little alphabet game. No one ever picked up on the fact that the first letter in the girl's name always matched the city and the first letter in his name matched the state. It was a silly little game he loved to play. He'd named it "Revenge on the Redheads" but, so far, no one had figured out that the seven women murdered in seven major cities were the work of one man.

His original plan was to do the entire alphabet but that became tiresome, if not impossible. He just did the best he could and only visited cities that interested him.

Alice in Atlanta, he was Greg. Bernice in Boston, he was Martin. Cindy in Chicago, he was Ian. Nancy in New Orleans, he was Larry. Dawn in Dallas, he was Troy. Linda in Los Angeles, he was Calvin and for pretty Penelope in Portland, he was Oakley.

Now he had Sheri in Seattle and it was time to put his plan into action.

"Sheri, this is Warren."

"Warren, it's nice to hear from you." He could hear the smile in her voice when she answered.

"I know this is a bit sudden, and I know how busy you are, but I was wondering if you'd like to come over to my house for dinner tonight. Cooking is a pretty big hobby of mine."

Her long pause did not bode well for the answer. He broke the silence.

"We've only had one lunch date so you're probably sitting there wondering how to gracefully decline. It's too soon, right? I thought so. It's just that I went to the Pike Street Market and bought some salmon and I don't want to freeze it."

Sheri laughed. "When I first came to Seattle, I was

a poor college student with a mini fridge and a microwave. It used to drive me crazy walking past all the fresh produce stalls in the market and seeing the seafood vendors, knowing I couldn't buy anything. The minute I was in my first apartment with a regular size refrigerator, I went nuts at the Market. I think I ate seafood every day for a week!"

Jon Albert loved inventing happy memories because he had none of his own. "When I was little my parents used to take me to the Pike Street Market every Saturday. We'd spend all morning there. My mom would haggle with the vendors for the best produce. My dad and I would walk along and take in the view of Puget Sound and the Olympic mountains. I loved all the noise and watching the tourists. Hard to believe it's been there for over a hundred years." He had an inspiration that he knew would pique her interest. "When I was first a rookie cop I used to patrol the market. I could tell you stories that would straighten your gorgeous, red curly hair!"

Sheri gave a little unladylike snort when she laughed. "You wouldn't believe how handy that would be sometimes. Men just don't understand what we go through for our hair!" Sheri paused again, mulling it over. "Okay Warren, this is only our second date and I have to let you know, don't expect anything from me but a good listener and a kitchen helper. This is way too soon for anything else. I'm going to make you swear on your badge that you will be a perfect gentleman."

Jon Albert pulled out his fake badge and smothered his laughter. Women were so predictable. "Okay, Sheri, it's in my hand. I swear I will be a perfect gentleman. And, just to put your mind at ease, I'll make sure it's an early night. I have church in the morning and I know you have a Seahawks game to cover. What time would you like me to pick you up?"

"No need to pick me up, I'll drive my own car."

He gave her directions and got off the phone. Jon Albert started whistling as he walked down the stairs to the little room behind the furnace. He unlocked the door and surveyed the interior. "Nice, this will do just fine." He turned a boom box on as loud as it would go, walked out of the room and shut the door.

"Ah, the sounds of silence. Nothing says love

quite like a soundproof room with lots of fun toys in it." He was almost giddy at the thought of what was to come.

Jon Albert opened the door to the soundproof room and walked back in. He took the boom box and flipped open the cassette holder. Preferring old technology to digital, he pulled out a box with seven cassettes marked with the name of each city he had visited. He was trying to decide which one would put him in the right mood. "Aha, I love Dawn from Dallas." He put the tape in, sat back in the only chair in the room and took a gentle float trip down memory lane.

The sound of Dawn's screaming filled the small room.

"Troy, why are you doing this? Please let me go, I promise not to tell anyone."

"It's a little too late for that, don't you think? Why do you women never pick up on clues? You deserve what you get." Jon Albert loved hearing them beg. He loved hearing the control in his voice. He was large and in charge.

"What are you doing?" Dawn stopped screaming

and he could hear the sound of her gulping a large quantity of air in disbelief.

Jon remembered how hard she thrashed around, more afraid of the hair clippers than of the array of knives on the nearby table.

The sound of a solid slap filled the room. "Shut up or I'll hurt you. Hold still or I'll slice that pretty face of yours."

"Please Troy, please. I'll do anything. Don't shave my head." Her plaintive pleas filled the room then and now.

The hair trimmers made an ominous sound as they dug into her long flowing red hair. Big chunks hit the floor like red streamers in a Chinese parade, the color celebratory against the dullness of the brown floor.

Jon Albert was visualizing how naked she had looked with her head shaved. He loved showing that he had total control of her. As he listened to the tape, his eyes wandered over to the shelf where he had seven bags of red hair on display. It almost brought tears to his eyes as he thought of his mother's glorious red hair.

Then his mind went back to the dark days and the things his mother had done to him.

Chapter 15

Sheri was tapping her foot on the floor. Impatience made a little crease in her otherwise smooth forehead. Her boss Russ was late for their meeting. She was sitting outside his office staring through the office window watching him and Dick Manson, the crime reporter. Sheri needed to get the go-ahead from Russ before she could meet with Trevor Long. Her meeting with Trevor was in an hour. At last, the two men stood up and Russ gestured for her to come in.

"Sorry to keep you waiting Sheri. Dick was just telling me about a story he's working on about a serial killer." Russ looked over at Dick and smiled.

Sheri let out an involuntary shudder and looked at Dick. "That really creeps me out. I remember when I saw pictures of Ted Bundy and Gary Ridgeway and how normal looking they were. Just makes you realize that a serial killer could be standing in line in front of you at the grocery store."

Analyzing murder was one of Dick's favorite pastimes and he loved the attention from the beautiful redhead. Dick was in his early forties and already his hair was three-quarters grey. Seeing the ugly side of life on a daily basis ages the soul and the body.

"Did you know they have traced serial killers back as far as 144 B.C.? There have been some real crazies in the world." Dick was just warming up to tell the history of serial killers when his phone beeped. He stopped to look at the message. "Well, this is pretty freaky. Speaking of serial killers, they found another body that I think ties into six other dead women. Penelope Johnston in Portland has been missing for four months. They just found her in a shallow grave outside of the city. That makes number seven."

Russ and Sheri's eyes got wide and they leaned in. Russ was the first to speak. "Are you going to tell us what's going on?"

Dick sat back down. "Like any reporter, I'm a news junkie. I started getting a funny feeling when two girls were murdered in separate cities and a few months apart. Here's the part that made my radar go off. They were both redheads and both of their heads had been shaved and the hair was never found."

Sheri's mouth opened and closed. As a redhead, she had heard all the myths and some of the crazy historical stuff about her hair color. "It sure wouldn't be the first time redheads were targeted. For instance, we've been targeted as witches and burned at the stake in more than one civilization and in multiple centuries. Hitler supposedly banned the marriages of redheads in order to prevent "deviant offspring." Eve was supposedly a brunette until she was cast out of the Garden of Eden, then she became a redhead. The list goes on and on."

Dick gave her a sympathetic look. "You're right, Sheri, but this is something pretty serious. I've been watching this for almost four years. The first two murders were a year apart. The next two were ten months apart and the last three have been less than five months apart. This guy is escalating. I've been passing my theory on to a local F.B.I. buddy of mine and they're watching this, too. Seven different states, seven young women with red hair, and all the deaths were brutal. The F.B.I. is calling him 'The Barber.' The last two were California and Oregon. Hopefully the guy isn't moving up to us."

"Dick, why hasn't there been any mention of this in the news? It's the first I've heard of a serial killer looking for redheads." Sheri shrugged and looked at her boss.

Dick picked up his thick file folder full of newspaper articles. "The F.B.I. is keeping a lid on this. They figure, based on his profile, the guy thinks he's smarter than everyone else and they don't want him to know they've seen his pattern. He's starting to get sloppy. He's cocky so he won't even imagine that anyone has figured it out."

He didn't get a chance to finish his comment when Sheri's cell phone started ringing. "Sorry Russ. I'll turn it off." She glanced at the caller ID and saw it was the Seattle Police Department calling. "Can I just take this call real fast? It could be about the attempted break-in at my house which works into the story I want to write."

Russ nodded and as Sheri walked out of the office the two men were deep in conversation.

"This is Sheri."

"Miss McLellon, this is Officer Davies. We met the other night when your alarm went off." His gravely voice sounded very formal.

"Yes Officer. Of course I remember. It's not every day something like that happens to me."

"I'm just trying to tie up some loose ends. You told me the other night that a police report had been written when your purse was taken. You said a Detective Trimble took the report?" Officer Davies paused. "I kind of have a thing about knowing all the cops at our local precincts. Heck, I know at least half of the ones downtown, too. The name Trimble didn't ring a bell with me but, like I said, I don't know everyone. After the odd day you had had, purse snatched, purse returned, house alarm goes off, something just didn't sit right with me. So I went to look for your police report and couldn't find it. I thought maybe it was in another precinct. To make a long story short, no report was ever filed. To really shake it up a bit, there is no officer named Trimble in the entire Seattle Police Department. Now Miss McLellon, are you one hundred percent positive he said Seattle?"

The color had drained out of Sheri's face and she sat down hard in a chair that was, thankfully, behind her or she would have hit the floor. "Yes, Officer Davies, I'm positive. What does this mean?"

"Sometimes you get a cop wannabe that pops up from time to time. For some reason, medical or mental, they can't make the force."

Sheri was stunned. And then a terrible realization hit her and her hands started to shake. "Officer Davies, I need to go. Can I call you back?"

"Are you all right? You sound funny."

"I just need to check on a few things. I'm okay." Sheri tried to make her voice normal but she just couldn't pull it off. "I'll call you back. Is the number in my phone a direct line or is there an extension."

"It's direct. Make sure you call me back."

"Yes, Officer." Sheri disconnected the call and her agile brain was racing through facts at record speed. On shaky legs, she walked back into her boss' office.

"Dick, I think you need to start at the beginning and tell me everything you know about this serial killer you're looking for. I may have some information that will help you."

Dick pulled out a sheath of papers and began his story. "Like I said, all redheads, all of their heads have been shaved, hair never found. They all were stabbed numerous times, a real indicator of the rage of the perp. I've got a list of the women. They were all in their middle to late twenties."

First	Last	City	State	Age
Alice	Middleton	Atlanta	Ga	28
Bernice	Nicely	Boston	Ma	29
Cindy	Jordan	Chicago	Il	23
Dawn	Jones	Dallas	Tx	26
Linda	Mosley	Los Angeles	Ca	25
Penny	Andrews	Portland	Or	27

Sheri looked at the list and let out a gasp. "Dick, did you notice how the first letter in the victim's first name is the same letter as the city?"

"I can't believe I missed something that obvious." Dick looked at the list and then the light bulb in his head went off. "Sheri from Seattle, is there something you need to tell me?"

Chapter 16

Trevor Long was frantically stuffing papers into his briefcase. He was rushing to meet Sheri for coffee when his phone rang.

"Hi Trevor, this is Sheri. I'm going to have to postpone our meeting today. Something's come up and I have to work." Sheri's voice was strained.

Trevor's radar went off. He chose his words carefully, wondering if she was on to him. "Are you all right? You sound upset. Is everything okay? If you want to change your mind about investing it's okay. I'd still like to see you."

Sheri didn't want to miss out on the chance of getting Trevor busted for attempted embezzlement. "No, honestly, I still want to discuss investments. I just can't do it today. You're leaving for the conference right? Call me when you get back and we'll set up another time."

Trevor mentally kicked himself for telling her he had a conference. Now it would be another four days of eating canned beans. He hated waiting. "I know you're busy but would you like me to drop the forms off at your house on my way to the airport?"

Sheri was losing patience and snapped. "Just call me when you get back. I have to go." She slammed the phone in his ear. Being stalked by a serial killer and a con man was beginning to get on her nerves.

Trevor held the phone out from his ear. "That bitch. She cancels and then slams the phone in my ear. This is total crap. I'm out of money and she's got a boat load of it. We're moving on to plan B."

Roger looked up from his Playboy magazine. "Plan B? I thought you had her right where you wanted her?"

Trevor walked over and got into Roger's face. "Don't you ever listen to me? She cancelled our coffee date. All the forms she was supposed to fill out now won't be done because I told her I was leaving town. I can't send you as my assistant because she might recognize you. It's blown. Totally blown. I can't wait four more days for money so we're going to break into her house and force her to do a wire transfer. Piece of cake. We'll poison her stupid animals and put a gun to her head."

"Dude, we don't have a gun."

Trevor smacked the top of Roger's head. "Yeah, I know that and you know that but she doesn't know that. We'll break-in in the middle of the night and grab her while she's sleeping. Who knows, maybe she even has some cash stashed at her house."

Roger started to perk up. "How are you going to get the she-devil cat to take your poison?"

I'll put it in some liver. I'll make a little meatball treat for both of those devil animals.

***

Ice was running in and out of the new doggie door.

"Come on, Cleo. This is fun. Watch me." Ice spun around and hit the door at a dead run. The little plexiglass door flipped open and he was off and running around the yard. Then he stopped, circled three times, and pooped in the yard. Business complete, he ran back into the house.

"Finished "thinking" Estupido?" Cleo yawned with boredom.

"Hey, it's a guy thing. I don't expect your highness to understand." Ice was in a foul mood. Sheri had been gone for three hours and it was the first time she hadn't taken him with her. She'd had a handyman install the dog door and left him stuck at home with Cleo.

"You're just being snippy because you're not in Sheri's purse."

"I'm 'snippy' as you call it because she's in danger and we finally know who's to blame. I should have known there was something off about Warren." Ice was pacing as he talked. As he circled back again to the dog door he heard a noise. *"Shhh. Cleo get over here. Someone's back by the fence."*

Cleo hated being bossed around but this was an extreme situation. She carefully got off the sofa and made her way over to Ice who was standing by the dog door. Both animals peered through the plexiglass trying to make out what was going on. They saw two round objects thrown over the fence and land with a "plop" onto the grass.

Cleo whispered to Ice, *"What is that?"* She pushed

the flap on the plexiglass and got a whiff of liver. *"It's food. Some nice neighbor is giving us a treat. I bet it's Mr. Johnstone next door. He's always telling me how beautiful I am."* Cleo pushed through the door and ran excitedly over to the food.

"No, Cleo, no." Ice ran straight at Cleo and body slammed her just as she was about to bite down on the food. *"Cleo, it's poison. I can smell ass man and that idiot Trevor's scent on it. Don't eat it."*

"Poison?" Cleo did a delicate sniff of the meat and stepped back. *"Do you think they're watching?"*

"They could be. Now this is important. I need you to grab the meat and carry it into the house. I'll grab this one. Don't swallow and try just to grab a little piece of it. We'll run into the house and if they're watching it will look like we're all excited about the treat. In fact, just to have a little fun, I'll move towards yours and you take a little swat at me."

Cleo perked up. *"I get to swat you? That almost, but not quite, makes up for the fact that I can't eat this little morsel. Okay, get ready."*

Cleo arched her back and let out a terrific howl. She did one of her ninja moves and, before Ice knew it, he actually did get smacked. Ice yelped and the squeaky sound made him see red. He was just about ready to go after Cleo when she actually winked at him, grabbed the meatball and ran back into the house through the dog door. Ice ran around the yard, pretending to sniff out the second piece of meat when he heard some muffled laughter in the bushes behind the fence. He could hear Trevor say something to ass man and then both men laughed.

Ice picked up the piece of meat and ran back into the house.

"Ptew. This is gross." Cleo spit the piece of meat onto the kitchen floor and watched as Ice did the same thing.

"Cleo, good job out there. You had me going for a minute. I thought you were trying to kill me." Ice stroked her ego and heard her purring.

"I am a natural, aren't I? Really, there should be more animal movies. Maybe we could do a remake of "Homeward Bound" and in this version, you'd be the animal that doesn't make it back."

"Yeah Cleo baby, I love you too. Now we have to get rid

of these meatballs. Can you jump up and put them in the garbage disposal?"

"Eww, you mean put them back in my mouth again?"

"I think you'll be fine. They always put the poison in the middle so just be careful."

As Cleo got rid of the second meatball they both heard the sound of a key in the front door. Ice and Cleo froze in place when two strangers with guns drawn walked into the house. Ice could see a radio ear-bud and their black suits screamed TV F.B.I. agents. He almost laughed at the stereo-type when the taller one said, "Go check the bedrooms. I'll do this part of the house." Just as Ice was about to bark and bite, the man spoke again. "Tell Miss McLellon I have eyes on two pets. They're fine. She'll see them as soon as we clear the house."

"Cleo, did you hear that? The Calvary has arrived. These must be the good guys."

"Estupido, as fond as I am growing of you, I just want this to end." A big tear started to fall down Cleo's face. *"I just want Sheri to be safe and for things to go back to normal."*

Ice walked over to the big mound of fur and ran his tongue over her face. *"Cleo, I know you're a big softie but your secret is safe with me. When I come back as myself, I'm going to bring you some nice liver meatballs to make up for the ones we had to throw away. It will all be ok."*

***

As Ice comforted Cleo, Sheri was brought in by the third F.B.I. man. She went over to the chair that Ice and Cleo were sharing and picked them both up and placed them on her lap as she sat down. Taking a minute to snuggle each of them, she tried to get her emotions under control.

"Okay Miss McLellon, we need a few minutes to strategize here. It looks like you've won the criminal lotto with not one, but two, possibly three bad guys targeting you. First order of business, you need to call Warren and cancel your date for tonight. We do not want you going into his house. It's too dangerous. If you cancel, it will probably lure him over to your house to make his move. We've got three F.B.I. agents that will stay at your house and one that will be doing surveillance of his house. If he moves this way, we'll know it."

Sheri nodded. She was pale but looked at the

F.B.I. agent with determination. "I will do anything I can to get this creep put away for life."

Agent Sellick gave her an encouraging smile. "That's the way. You're a brave woman and what you're doing here tonight will save the lives of other women. Guys like this don't just stop, they have to be stopped."

Sheri picked up her phone and when all three agents were in the room, Agent Sellick gave her the nod.

She heard his phone ring and braced herself when he answered. "Warren, this is Sheri. I'm so sorry but I have to cancel this evening. I'm kind of embarrassed about the reason."

Warren's voice was strained when he asked, "But you told me you could make it. What happened?"

"Oh, Warren, I was really looking forward to coming over tonight but I was doing some yard work and I disturbed a bees' nest. Apparently they are not quite ready for hibernation because I have several stings and had an allergic reaction. My doctor gave me a pretty strong shot of Benadryl and it will probably knock me out for the evening. Last time this happened and I got a shot, I slept like the dead for eighteen hours."

The disappointment disappeared from Warren's voice and he struggled to keep his enthusiasm under control. "Oh, well, I understand. Tell you what, I'll freeze the salmon and we can have it this week. I'm so sorry you're going through this. You must really have a sensitivity to Benadryl for it to knock you out like that. I'll call you tomorrow to see how you're doing."

"Thanks, Warren. Have a good night."

Sheri hung up the phone and the agent called Young burst out laughing. "Seriously? You said 'slept like the dead' to a serial killer? Talk about a fucking sick sense of humor, if you don't mind me saying."

Agent Sellick frowned at Young. "Language, Agent Young."

Sheri laughed. "Please, Agent Sellick, I grew up in Minnesota hanging out in hockey rinks. If you think that's the worst I've ever heard, you are sadly mistaken."

At the mention of hockey, Ice scooted over closer and gave her hand a lick. It was killing him that he couldn't hold her and give her comfort.

Sheri patted the little dog and looked at the agent in charge. "What's the plan?"

"If our hunch about Warren Trimble is correct, he's not going to like being deprived of seeing you and fulfilling his plan. Sorry to be so blunt but I think it was you on the menu for tonight, not the salmon."

"Yes, I gathered that by all of the information my colleague, Dick Manson, gave me before he called you."

Sheri stared at the three men in her house. Agent Sellick looked like he was about fifty with a full head of grey hair. His face had frown lines etched into the sides of his mouth and permanent dark circles under his brown eyes clearly said this man had seen too much of the seamier side of life. He'd been chasing the "Barber Killer" since the third victim and it was wearing him down.

"He usually manages to lure the women to his home which suggests to me he has some sort of room set up. Otherwise, he would have killed the women in their own homes. From interviewing family and friends of the victims, all of the woman had recently started dating a new man. And, as you so astutely pointed out, he also has an alphabet thing going on. This man's criminal profile is classic. I'm willing to bet he has huge mommy issues."

Agent Young thought Sheri was pretty cute. He was twenty-nine and still a rookie. The F.B.I. had been a lifelong dream and he'd sacrificed a social life to get there. He was trying to figure out how to engage her in conversation when he looked at the animals in Sheri's lap. "Too bad you don't have a bigger dog for protection, and the cat's sure as heck not going to do much. Good thing you've got us to guard you."

Ice turned around, bared his teeth and a deep, low growl came out. Cleo fluffed up her tail and hissed at the agent. Sheri laughed out loud. "Well, Agent Young, you sure know how to get on the wrong side of my meek, mild little animals. If I were you, I'd give these two a wide berth. They are very protective of me."

***

Ice was pissed but pretty pleased about how good he was getting at growling.

"Did you hear me, Cleo? That was my best growl yet. I'm getting good at this dog thing." Ice's little dog chest puffed up with pride.

"Estupido, you'd better be good at a whole lot more than

growling. This F.B.I. kid is going to be useless. The old dude looks worn out. And the third one hasn't uttered a word since he got here."

Ice looked at the men in the room. *"Well, Cleo baby, glad you've got my back because, I agree. When the shit hits the fan, these three better stay out of our way. Come on, we need to check out Sheri's bedroom and play dead on the floor."*

***

"Miss McLellon, I'm turning off all the lights in the house. We've got Agent Young in your bedroom closet, I'm by the front door and Monroe will take the back door. We'll be ready when the suspect makes his move. We have an agent with eyes on that will alert us when he leaves his house.

It was ten o'clock and Sheri was tired. Who knew that being a target could be so exhausting. "So, I'm just supposed to get in bed and go to sleep? Right, like that's going to happen."

"Well, not exactly. I do have a few tricks up my sleeve." Sellick opened a large canvas bag and pulled out a long red haired wig and another object. "Young, blow this up for me."

Young got red-faced from the effort but finally the shape of a woman started to form.

Sheri's jaw dropped. "You brought a blow-up doll to take my place?"

"We just want to have a decoy and, since red hair is the trigger, I brought the wig. We want you to be safe so you'll stay out in the living room with me. Okay people, everyone in their place. I don't expect any action until at least midnight but better safe than sorry. Miss McLellon, do you want to get a blanket from your bedroom?"

"Sure. And while I'm at it I'll put our little friend here in bed." Sheri grabbed the blow-up doll and walked down the dark hallway guided by the night-lights. After grabbing a blanket and placing the doll in the bed, Sheri looked down and could just make out the outline of Pablo and Cleo. They looked dead to the world.

***

Cleo hissed into Ice's ear. *"You're such a ham. Do you really think when dogs die their legs are straight up in the air?"*

"How am I supposed to know? Now shut up so I can listen." Ice whispered back.

As Cleo was about to smack Ice, they both heard a noise. Ice thought frantically, *this can't be Warren. The Feds didn't get the call that he'd left his house.*

The window started to open and Ice and Cleo watched as two black-clad figures climbed into the room. Ice looked at Cleo, freezing her in place with a look. He wanted to make sure they were far enough from the window that they couldn't make a sudden retreat. As the men inched towards the bed, Ice gave his battle cry and both animals sprung into action.

Cleo went for the first head she could get her paws on and Ice kept his signature move of biting a big piece of someone's ass. The screams from the men were loud and Young burst out of the closet, gun drawn, as Monroe and Sellick flipped on the lights with their guns drawn.

The sight would have been comical if not for the big knife in Trevor's hand and the handcuffs and duct tape in Roger's hand. Trevor was wearing Cleo like a raccoon hat. Her claws were embedded into the side of his head and her teeth were grabbing an eyebrow. Blood was pouring out of the wound and Trevor was screaming like a little girl.

Roger had Ice on his ass again and was spinning around trying to throw him off. Ice clamped down harder and growled.

Trevor screamed at Roger, "I told you it wasn't enough poison, you asshole."

Sheri came into the room as the agents had the two men on the floor. She managed to get Cleo and Ice to disengage. As she held them both, she smothered them with kisses cooing, "My brave, brave babies. You saved the day."

Agent Sellick was on the phone to the Seattle Police Department to come book and transport the bungling burglars. A quick search of their pockets yielded a bank account number for the Caymen Islands and step-by-step instructions on how to transfer money to the bank. The duct tape, handcuffs and big kitchen knife showed how desperate Trevor had become.

Agent Sellick was the first to speak. "Miss McLellon, this is the guy you told me about? The one that went to the minimum security prison for embezzlement?"

"Yes, he's the one. I can't believe he tried to poison my animals."

"Well, sadly, we can't get him on attempted murder of your pets but we can get him on felony charges for possession of a weapon. That will get him sent away to a lovely prison with guys named Bubba instead of a minimum security facility. He's going to regret this evening every day for years to come."

Sheri looked at Trevor with his hands cuffed behind him and blood running down his face from Cleo's attack. "You didn't fool me. Not for one minute. You're a lousy con artist and embezzler. And, you're not that good looking."

Trevor's face contorted in anger. "You're on your way to becoming the crazy cat lady and if you didn't have all that money, no one would look at you."

The minute he said that, Ice was up and charging. He went straight for the front section of Trevor's pants and bit as hard as he could. The high pitched scream from Trevor told him he'd hit his target. He kept biting right up to the point when Trevor fainted.

Agent Young walked over to Ice. "Ok Pablo,

good dog. Good job. You got him and you saved your owner." He looked over at Sheri and said, "I will never make fun of little dogs again, or cats either. You have a pair of kick-ass protectors."

Roger looked over at Trevor laying on the floor. "This is your fault. You never listen to me. Now we'll both be someone's bitch."

***

Officer Davies came through the front door with another uniformed police officer. He headed straight to Sheri. "Miss McLellon, you didn't call me back. When I saw the call come through for your address I figured I'd come see what's up."

For some reason, the deep gravely voice and the concern in his eyes made Sheri's eyes tear up. "I'm okay. I'm apparently the flavor of the month on the embezzlers' and serial killers' hit list."

Officer Davies looked over her head at Agent Sellick. "That true?"

Sellick sighed, "Yes, unfortunately, it is. These guys were a bonus, we weren't expecting them tonight. Officer, I need you to get these guys out of here, throw them in a cell and we'll come do the paperwork in the morning. It's imperative that we get back to the business of catching the serial killer that has targeted Miss McLellon."

"I know you Feds think you have it all handled, but you better make doubly sure with this one. I've grown quite fond of Sheri McLellon and her animals. You sure you don't need an extra guy?"

Sheri smiled and then watched as Pablo went up and wagged his tail at the officer.

Sellick was getting antsy. "OK, guys, get these two losers out of here and its back to waiting." As he spoke, his radio crackled.

"Sellick, he's on the move."

"Everyone out now. Suspect just left his house. We've got about twenty minutes. Young, back in the closet. Sheri, you're in the living room with me. Monroe, back door. Now, people, get in position."

Everyone scrambled and the two cops grabbed Trevor and Roger. Ice gave one last growl at Trevor and did a great dog sneer when he saw Trevor tremble in fear.

Chapter 17

Jon Albert Culver was flying high. He loved the rush he got before he brought a girl home. Grabbing Sheri from her house was not the normal modus operandi he worked under, but he knew as "Warren the cop" he would pull it off. He navigated the streets carefully. At 2 a.m., he was on the lookout for drunks or cops.

His thoughts were on all that luscious red hair. Hair just like his mother's only this time he could touch the hair as much as he wanted. He wouldn't get slapped and punished for touching her hair with dirty hands.

Pulling the car into the dark alley behind Sheri's house, he looked at the neighborhood. He had done this several times and knew he would be able to spot a car out of place. He was relieved that Sheri was probably sound asleep on Benadryl. It would make things so much easier. He reached across the seat of his car and pulled out his dart gun. He would rather shoot to kill the little rat dog but didn't have a silencer for his gun. Tranquilizer darts would have to do. Jon Albert had a thought, *maybe I should kidnap the dog too. I'd love to kill that little mutt.*

He got out of the car, silent as the night, and carefully opened the back gate to Sheri's yard. His movements were stealth under the moonless skies and he walked with purpose, his night vision goggles guiding the way. All of a sudden his nostrils were filled with a pungent odor. Cursing, he knew he'd hit poop from the damn dog. Silently scraping his shoe in the grass, he was thankful that Pedro wasn't a Great Dane. He mused, little dog, little shit. Could have been worse.

Finally standing under Sheri's window he listened carefully. There was no sound. The household was asleep. Carefully sliding the window up, he crawled inside, his eyes taking in the bedroom scene as Sheri slept soundly on the bed. Jon Albert could see she hadn't moved a muscle, the Benadryl doing its job and helping him out. Her face was covered by her hair and as he approached the bed he grabbed a handful of it and pulled her head back, his knife under her chin. "Don't say a word or I'll slice you like a piece of pie." To emphasize his words, he dug the blade into her neck. The blow-up doll let out a rush of air and, despite his grasp on her hair, the doll flew off the bed and collapsed. Jon Albert was left holding a red-headed wig and when the lights suddenly came on, he was surrounded by three men with guns drawn. He pulled out the tranquilizer gun and aimed for the biggest of the three. His shot went astray but the F.B.I.'s didn't. Searing pain hit him in his shoulder and he fell backwards onto the floor. The tranquilizer gun was kicked out of his hand and he felt something tugging at his pants leg and then more pain as the little Chihuahua's teeth sunk deep into his ankle.

***

Ice was holding onto "Warren" with a death grip and could feel the blood rushing into his mouth. Then he felt a violent jerk as "Warren" kicked his leg into the air and Ice was airborne, crashing into the wall by Sheri's bed.

Sellick yelled out to Sheri, "We have him secured. You can come in."

Sheri walked into the bedroom. The man she knew as Warren was face down on the floor, his hands cuffed behind him. Young picked him up and Monroe grabbed the other side. When Warren looked at Sheri his eyes glazed over. "So, beautiful. We could have had so much fun together. I wanted your hair for my collection."

"You're a sick individual and I hope they put you away for a thousand years." Sheri looked at him with well-deserved scorn and continued. "I don't care what kind of problems you've had in your life. It doesn't give you the right to kill innocent women."

Warren's face shifted and the mask came off. "You're all bitches. Controlling, evil bitches. I'm just sorry they caught me before I got to you. And I hope I killed your stupid dog."

Young and Monroe pulled him out of the room. A car was in route to take them all the police station. Once he was deposited, the rest of the night would be spent searching his home.

***

Sheri turned to Agent Sellick and tried to smile. "Thank

you. I don't know that I'll get any sleep for awhile but it feels good knowing that this guy is going to pay for what he's done. He looked so normal. I may have to join a nunnery after this experience. My trust factor is really low right now."

"Miss McLellon, you're a beautiful, smart, talented woman. If you let this ruin the rest of your life then that scumbag wins. You're better than that. Now, is there someone I can call to come stay with you?"

"Thanks, but I can make the call. I think you would scare the life out of my best friend if you started the call with 'This is Agent Sellick from the F.B.I.' She knows that Trevor has been up to no good but this whole thing with Warren, or whatever his name is, happened so fast I didn't get a chance to call her."

"Call her now and I'll wait until she gets here before I leave."

***

Cleo was panicked. She ran into Sheri's bedroom and saw the little dog lying on the floor. *"Estupido, wake up, wake up."* She nudged him with her head and no response. Then she heard a scream from Sheri. "Pablo!"

The little Chihuahua didn't move. Tears were streaming down Sheri's face as she gently stroked his head, willing him to wake up.

Cleo looked up and saw Uncle Tony and let out a cat shriek. *"Help him, help Ice."*

Uncle Tony looked at Cleo. "It's all right, baby girl. Everything is going to be all right. Ice is gone but just from this little guy's body."

"But, Uncle Tony, I didn't get a chance to say good-bye."

"I have a funny feeling you'll get that chance. Take care of Sheri." Uncle Tony disappeared and Cleo howled again.

The little dog jumped up at the sound. *"Donde estoy? Quien es esta Hermosa diosa delante de mi?"*

Cleo stared at the dog. Her big eyes had a look of disbelief. *"The question, you ugly little dog, is who are you? Not who are we!"*

"You speak English? Where am I? My name is Louie."

Cleo decided that it wasn't this ugly little mutt's fault he got caught up in all this drama. *"You're at our house. We live near Green Lake on 48th, just off Aurora. Do you live near here?"*

"Hey gorgeous, we're neighbors. My people live on 49th, just off Stoneway North. How long have I been here? My Lola is going to be worried."

Cleo thought to herself, *just long enough for me to learn to love you.* Instead she said, *"About two weeks."*

"I gotta get out of here. My people must be looking for me." The little dog was looking around for an exit when they both heard the doorbell ring.

"Oh, boy, I know what that means. That door is about to open and I'm out of here. My Lola needs me. Hasta la vista, baby."

The little dog ran towards the sound like the devil was behind him. As Johnni opened the front door, the dog ran out into the night, stopped to sniff the air and ran towards home.

Chapter 18

Ice woke up with a start. His eyes were blurry and he couldn't focus. He felt someone grab his hand and take his pulse. His lips were chapped but he managed to talk. "Where am I? Is Sheri okay?"

"Mr. Zamboni, you're awake! Let me just ring for your doctor." The nurse pushed a call button and spoke, "Get Doctor Lewis, Mr. Zamboni just woke up."

Ice still couldn't see and was starting to panic.

"Mr. Zamboni, I'm going to wipe your eyes for you. They're covered in Vaseline to keep them from drying out. You've been in a coma for almost two weeks and sometimes they would just pop open but, to be blunt, no one was home. Then I'm going to go out to the waiting area. You have some family members that I promised to let know when you woke up."

The nurse placed a warm wet washcloth on his

eyes and gently removed the film. Ice could see clearly and was just a little freaked out when he spotted his uncle Tony sitting on the end of the bed staring at him.

The nurse exited the private room and Ice looked at his uncle. "Is Sheri okay? Did it work?"

Uncle Tony gave a wide smile in answer. "Kid, you were fantastic. Actually, you were fearless. You saved the day and the big Guy is pleased. Normally, when something like this happens, we erase your memory of it. But…like I said, some of those angels owe me so I'm just going to slip out of here and leave you to think things over. See you in another fifty or sixty years."

Uncle Tony vanished and Ice was left to think about everything that had happened. It was all pretty confusing but the one thing he knew for certain was he had to get back to Sheri. He wasn't going to lose her again.

For the next hour, his nurse brought family members in to see him. There were a lot of tears from his mom and he even saw his old man wipe his eyes. His mom couldn't stand it any longer, "Jeffrey Andrew

Zamboni, you have to mend your ways. You can't keep using women the way you do. I knew something like this was going to happen one day."

"Relax mom. I get it, I finally get it. Believe me, I won't take advantage or use women again. I'm ready to settle down."

His parents both said at once. "Not with the crazy woman that shot you?"

Ice almost laughed at the thought but remembered he was turning over a new leaf. "No, you can rest your minds on that. I'm going to make you proud, I promise."

As his parents were leaving, Ice was almost ready to drift off to sleep when a familiar face stood by the bottom of his bed.

Peter Arnstrom looked at Ice tentatively. "Hey big guy, how you doing? I called your cell phone and your mom filled me in. I got here yesterday."

Ice decided to cut to the chase. "So, it wasn't just some crazy dream was it? I feel like Dorothy waking up with the Scarecrow, Tinman and Lion all staring at me. Last time I saw you, you were changing the locks at

Sheri's. You knew it was me didn't you? How'd you know?"

"Yeah, I kind of figured it out. Of course, you dragging a picture of yourself out helped too. I'll tell you how I knew but if you tell anyone I will call you crazy and have you locked up. My mom is Swedish and they call her a häxa which is Swedish for witch. She's really not a witch. You've met her. She's actually pretty cool, but she has this weird ability to communicate with animals. I kind of inherited part of it."

Peter was actually blushing. "This is so embarrassing. I could hear you at Sheri's, but there was no way I was going to tell her. Besides, all I could hear was you whining about having tiny balls. Really Ice, all you could come up with was 'What happened to my balls?'

Ice looked down at his crotch. "I haven't checked; hopefully I didn't keep the Chihuahua's balls. It was really scary to look at my dog equipment."

Peter rolled his eyes and continued. "I was still trying to figure out what was going on when the shit hit the fan. Looking at you now, you should have stayed a dog. You're looking a little rough around the edges."

"Being shot will do that to you. And then, being kicked into a wall. Hope the little mutt whose body I borrowed is okay."

Peter almost laughed at the absurdity of the situation. "Ice, how in the heck did you end up in an ugly little Chihuahua's body?

"Bad karma and as my long dead uncle, who is now an angel, told me, "The Big Guy has a sense of humor." I guess it was my last chance to redeem myself for not treating Sheri right when we were in high school and for being an idiot. Oh, and as my uncle told me, living a shallow life. Is she okay? The last thing I remember is them handcuffing the guy named Warren."

"Warren turned out to be a guy named Jon Albert Culver. He had killed seven women and Sheri would have been number eight. When they searched his house they found some pretty gruesome stuff. He was, excuse the expression, one sick puppy."

"I was so distracted by that idiot Trevor at first I didn't even suspect Warren. He seemed a little off but nothing that stuck out. Then I smelled his scent outside of Sheri's bedroom window and knew he was the danger."

"From what the press has said, serial killers are very intelligent and able to blend into society. Pretty scary. The press is having a field day. They've dubbed him "The Barber" because he cut off all of the victim's hair."

Ice gave an involuntary shudder. "This whole thing creeps me out. Poor Sheri. Not one, but two crazies after her."

"Aww, come on Ice, don't be so hard on yourself. I wouldn't call you a crazy." Peter did his best to keep a straight face.

"Don't make me laugh. I still have stitches that hurt. You know I'm coming to Seattle the minute they let me out of here. I've wasted too many years not seeing her and now I know, after spending time with Sheri, she's the woman I want forever."

"Really? She could communicate with you in dog language?" Peter was okay with it but the whole situation was a little absurd. "You plan on winning her heart? Last time I talked to her she could barely say your name without wanting to spit on the floor."

"Yeah, about that. I have some making up to do. It's been ten years and we're both different people. Well, I'm different now. Getting shot, turning into a dog and getting beaten up by a cat can really change a person." Ice shrugged his shoulders, "What can I say? She had me at 'Here, doggie.'"

Peter laughed. "Ice, you're one of my best friends. I'll help you anyway I can."

"Yeah, animal whisperer, it's not the cat I'm worried about, it's getting Sheri to forgive me."

Chapter 19

Sheri was in a funk. It had been raining men and now it was a drought. Not that she'd been looking. It was the last thing on her mind. Johnni had tried to get her to go out for their usual girl's night but Sheri refused. When her cell phone rang again, she jumped. Her nerves were on edge.

"Miss McLellon, this is Agent Sellick. I wanted to catch you up-to-date on what's going on with your fan club." He bit back a laugh at his little joke.

"Agent Sellick, that's not funny. Maybe someday I'll find some humor in this but it won't be in the near future."

"I'm sorry, it's cop humor. We're always a little on the dark side. Anyway, the two suspects, Trevor Long and Roger Williams were unable to post bail and are in the county jail. They will be arraigned tomorrow and their court date will be set. I'd guess, with the courts as backed up as they are, that they'll be sitting in jail for at least six months before they see a courtroom. You will be called upon to testify and the prosecuting attorney will contact you."

"I'll be happy to help put those two in prison and hopefully throw away the key. The two of them are both so stupid that they are a danger to themselves and the rest of us."

"You're absolutely correct. I'm positive that Trevor won't be sitting in a cushy minimum security prison this time. The other guy, Roger, might not get much time. He wasn't the mastermind to all this."

"I keep seeing that knife in Trevor's hand. I guess I have to be grateful that a serial killer was after me too or you guys wouldn't have been there to save the day." The relief in Sheri's voice was evident.

"That's kind of a weird silver lining isn't it? I'm glad we were there. I'm sorry that your little dog ran off. He was a good protector."

A tear slid down Sheri's cheek. "Hopefully he's found his home. I checked on Craigslist and there was an ad for a lost Chihuahua near Green Lake that was posted two days after I found him. I'm sure it was for Pablo. Things escalated so fast with my "fan club" that I hadn't looked. Hopefully, when he ran out the door, it was for home."

"Animals and people come into our lives for a reason. Maybe saving you was Pablo's job and he succeeded." Agent Sellick was getting philosophical in his old age.

Sheri was finding the talk about Pablo depressing and wanted to get off the phone. "Agent Sellick, I have to go. My friend Johnni is coming over for dinner."

After saying their goodbyes, Sheri hung up the phone and went in search of Cleo. She found her right where she had been for the last month. Sleeping on the bed right where Pablo had slept.

Chapter 20

Ice got off the plane at Seattle Tacoma International Airport. He was so anxious to get to Sheri's that he'd packed only a carry-on bag, not willing to waste time waiting for his luggage. It was exactly a month since he'd seen her. The doctors had been insistent that he wait until he was given a clean bill of health before he could board a plane.

Standing in line at the queue for the taxi he noted the night air was chilly. Not Minnesota chilly but with the dampness in the air he could feel his cheeks getting red. Finally getting into the cab, he gave the driver Sheri's address. He kept trying to think of what he was going to say to her and hoped she'd give him the chance to explain everything.

The cab pulled into her driveway and Ice got out with his duffle bag. Taking a deep breath, he walked up to the front door and rang the bell.

The door opened and he stood staring at a tall, beautiful woman who

was not Sheri.

Johnni looked Ice up and down and said, "I've ordered pizza delivered but have never had a fine looking man delivered before. What's your name handsome?"

Ice watched her eyes go big when he said his name.

"Seriously, *the* Ice??? Get yourself in here right now. I want to see the look on Sheri's face when she sees you. It's about time you showed up."

"I would have been here a lot sooner but the doctors wouldn't release me."

Johnni looked at him closely. "Please dear God, tell me you're talking medical doctors and not crazy in the head doctors. We've had enough crazy around here to last a lifetime."

Ice had the good grace to look embarrassed. "Well it was kind of crazy. Lady I was dating shot me. And to set the record straight, she was crazy, she's in jail and it was medical doctors that were slow on letting me out of the hospital."

Johnni impulsively hugged him. "I have a feeling that you are here for awhile and that you and I are going to be very good friends because we both love Sheri."

"I'm that obvious? I don't want to scare her off." Ice was worried. He had arrived without a plan and now this woman was seeing right through him.

"Honey, your secret is safe with me. Just promise me you won't do anything stupid and break her heart." Johnni had her hands on her hips and gave him a glare and added. "Again."

"I promise. I want to make up for the past and start over." Ice's big brown eyes looked at Johnni pleadingly.

All of a sudden there was the sound of glass breaking. They both turned around to see that Sheri had dropped a tray full of drinks onto the stone tiled entryway.

"Ice? Oh my God. What are you doing here? Are you okay? I heard about you being shot." Sheri was rushing towards Ice as she fired questions at him.

When she got close enough, Ice reached out and grabbed her in a massive hug. He breathed in deeply the scent of her hair and the smells of home. "God I've missed you. I'm so sorry I was such an ass on prom night."

Sheri disengaged from the hug. "Ice, in the last month I've had my life threatened by a serial killer and two bumbling embezzlers were after me. Life got put into perspective and your little stunt was just an eighteen year-old boy trying to get laid on prom night. Believe me, I'm over it."

"Sheri, I'm so sorry for all that you've been through and I'm still sorry about prom night. I can't tell you how many thousands of times I've regretted that mistake."

"Ice, it's okay. Come in and sit down while I clean up the mess I just made."

"Let me help. It's my fault for showing up unannounced."

"No, please just go sit in the living room. This will only take a couple of minutes. What would you like to drink when I refill everything? Beer? Wine?"

"A beer would be great." Ice walked into the living room as Sheri and Johnni walked into the kitchen. He sat on the sofa when Cleo sauntered into the room, stopped dead in her tracks, and let out a long meow. *"Is it you? Is it really you?"* And then she launched herself into his lap.

Ice whispered in her ear. "Shhh It's me. Cleo baby, don't blow my cover. She'll never believe our story."

Cleo started to purr and looked up at Ice with adoring eyes. Sheri walked in with their drinks and exclaimed, "Cleo, you're up and you're purring!"

Ice kept a neutral look on his face. "She sure is a friendly cat and such a beauty."

"You don't understand. She's been lethargic for the last month and has barely eaten. I practically have to force her to eat. She got attached to a little Chihuahua I adopted. The dog ran off and she's been despondent. My poor baby."

Cleo's purr was as loud as a jet engine. "I don't believe this. She hasn't moved from the bedroom since Pablo ran off."

"Tell her I'm hungry." Cleo demanded.

Ice thought to himself, *jeez, not here ten minutes and already she's bossing me around. Might as well get used to it.* "She looks like she's hungry. If you get some food I'll feed her."

"I don't remember you as being a big animal lover Ice." Sheri looked at her old friend with a perplexed expression.

"Sheri, you wouldn't believe how attached I've become to animals. See even Cleo recognizes an animal lover."

***

Sheri walked into the kitchen to get Cleo some food and Johnni was right on her heels.

"Girl, you did not tell me the man is eye candy on a platter." Johnni smacked her lips for good measure.

Sheri's eyes lit up. "He does look good, doesn't he? A little skinnier than I remember but I think it was from being in the hospital and in a coma."

Johnni narrowed her eyes and gave Sheri the truth or die look. "So, you knew about his coma and being shot? You never said a word to me about it. What gives?"

"I didn't want to look like a cyber stalker. I couldn't help myself. I've been googling him since Google became the cyber stalker's best friend. I just wanted to know what he was up to." Sheri's face was beet red and she was trying to get Johnni to change the subject. "What time is Peter coming over?"

"Nice try but we're not finished with this conversation, and it is long overdue. I can't believe you didn't tell me all this! So what did you learn about him?"

Sheri mumbled. "He turned out to be a really nice guy. He donates a lot of time and money to help women's shelters and homeless people. And, he's never had a serious girlfriend." She paused to add, "Ever. They call him the three date wonder. I guess that's why the last one shot him."

Johnni couldn't help the giggle that escaped. "That is so harsh. I mean, I've had men in my life that I would have loved to shoot. I wonder how it feels to actually do it?"

Sheri shuttered. "It was awful to read about. He almost died. I'm so happy he's okay."

"Yeah, I bet you are. Especially since the first place he landed out of the hospital was on your front porch. I think that man is looking to break the three date rule and it's about time you did too." Johnni put on her sternest look.

"Let's get back in there before Cleo shows her true colors and scratches him."

***

Sheri picked up the bowl of cat food and walked back into the living room. Cleo looked up from Ice's lap and stopped mid-purr.

"Well, since she's brought me food, I guess I could force a little down. Ice, help me eat." Cleo looked up at Ice and gave him a little wink.

Ice looked down at the cat and patted her head. "Poor little Cleo. Maybe you should get her another dog to hang out with."

Cleo jumped up and her tail spiked out and her back arched. *"Well, that's a fine way to treat an old friend. Sheri better not drag home another sorry-looking animal. You're lucky I put up with you and didn't eat you the first night."*

Sheri watched the interaction between her cat and Ice. "This is so weird. It sounds like she's talking to you. She did the same thing with Pablo."

"She is quite the talker." Ice couldn't take his eyes off Sheri. "Come and sit down so we can catch up on the last ten years." Ice patted the spot next to him and was relieved when Sheri sat next to him.

"So you're a big time sports reporter. I know I'll sound like some sort of cyber-stalker but I read your column all the time." Ice was confused when both Sheri and Johnni choked on their drinks.

Johnni recovered first. "Cyber stalker, what an interesting term. What else did you look up on our little Sheri?"

Ice turned to Sheri and took her hand. "I've wanted to come and see you for years. When I woke up from my coma and read that a serial killer had been stalking you, I couldn't get here fast enough. If anything had happened to you I would have never forgiven myself."

Sheri smiled and felt the ice around her heart melt. "What are your plans? How long are you in town for?" She held her breath as she waited for his answers.

"I'm thinking of relocating to Seattle. Peter Arnstrom has been after me to come out and help him with his group of boys. I'll be staying with Peter, who I understand lives pretty close to you?"

"He lives in Ballard. That neighborhood is about

fifteen minutes from here. My neighborhood is called Greenwood. Ballard is a Scandinavian neighborhood, or at least that's how it started out. It's right by the water and lots of fishermen lived there in the old days. That's the history I've been told."

"I'm looking forward to learning all about Seattle and its history, especially if I have you as a teacher. You always were the smarter one."

Sheri blushed with pleasure.

As they sat in the living room staring at each other and smiling, the doorbell rang.

Sheri jumped. "I'm not expecting anyone."

"It could be Peter. I told him I was coming here straight from the airport."

"I'll get it. You two just keep talking and gazing into each other's eyes." Johnni jumped up off the couch and headed for the front door.

"Open up, it's cold out here." Peter's voice was loud but Johnni could hear the laughter behind the words.

"Well, well, well. Look who shows up. Another mighty-fine looking man." Johnni smiled as Peter leaned in for a hug.

Sheri looked over at Peter. "Ice hasn't been here very long. What, do you have the place bugged or something? I need to train Cleo to sniff out bugs."

Peter said, "I knew what time his flight was getting in and, in case you were still mad at Ice, I wanted to get here before he froze to death on the curb."

Sheri laughed. After the month she'd had, it felt good to be surrounded by friends.

Ice looked down at Cleo who was drooling in his lap. "Wow, Peter, I think she's drooling even more than when she met you." The minute the words were out of his mouth he realized his mistake. He looked over at Peter who also looked like a deer in the headlights.

Sheri and Johnni looked at the two men. Ice thought quickly. "Peter told me about your cat, he was worried about my allergies. Told me what a beauty she was and how she drooled all over him when he came to change your locks."

Cleo was listening carefully and decided to throw in her two cents worth. She looked up at Ice and let out a long series of meows and growls. *"You're going to blow this Estupido. You better just fess up to everything. If she catches you in a lie, she'll never speak to you again. But then, if that happens, my place on the bed will be secure."*

Ice looked down at the cat and before he could stop himself he blurted out. "Cleo, it's not time to talk about that yet."

Sheri and Johnni exchanged looks of concern, with both their eyebrows shooting up to their hairline.

Sheri turned to Ice. "Any reason you're talking to my cat like a crazy person? And why on earth does it sound like she's answering you?"

Ice was speechless. He looked at Peter and saw his friend shrug his shoulders.

"Let me start at the beginning. Wait, let me start with how I've been wasting my life for the last ten years. I have never had a relationship longer than three dates in all these years. The women would bore me to tears by the third date." Ice took a deep breath, "Now I need to tell you what happened after the last woman I was with shot me on date number three."

Ice told her everything that had gone on when he was Pablo, stopping finally when he saw her frown and her eyes grew wide with disbelief.

"Did I miss the news story about you losing your mind? It sounds like you had some very vivid dreams when you were in your coma."

"Sheri, I swear to you, when I woke up in the hospital I knew it was all true. It's too crazy of a story for me to make up. How do you explain about Cleo knowing me? And I need to give Cleo something I promised her." Ice walked over to his duffle bag, opened it and pulled out a little baggie with meatballs.

"Cleo baby, I can't believe how much I missed you." Ice pulled out a liver meat ball and held it out to her. Even though you always called me Estupido, I know you love me." He looked at Sheri and added. "I promised her I'd bring her liver meat balls as a replacement for the poison ones that Trevor and his sidekick tried to get us to eat."

The cat leaned over and took a delicate bite out of the meatball. *"Oh Estupido, these are amazing."* Her purr was as loud as the crescendo in an Italian opera.

Sheri stood with her hands on her hips trying to decide what to do. She looked at Ice and said,

"Estupido?"

Ice decided to just let it fly and see what happened. "It's a long story but when you named me Pablo, Cleo decided to go with the Spanish word for stupid." He looked down at Cleo, "But its okay. I know she loves me."

Sheri was grasping at straws, not willing to believe any of his story.

"Oh my God! You saw me naked? You slept with me every night and listened in on my most private conversations? You pervert."

"Sheri, I know it sounds crazy and I'm really sorry about the seeing you naked part but there was nothing I could do about it."

"This is insane. You're insane. I guess I missed the news story about you losing your mind." Sheri was near tears. After the stress of being the "flavor of the month" for the serial killer and embezzlers, she was not about to listen to any of this nonsense.

"You need to go. Ice, I don't know what kind of game you're playing but I'm done with it."

Johnni jumped up. "Peter, I think you and your

friend need to leave. I'm going to talk Sheri off the cliff. We'll call you tomorrow."

Ice hung his head. How could it have gone wrong so quickly. Cleo shot him a sympathetic look and then jumped down and rubbed against his legs.

Sheri looked at Cleo. "Get back over here you little traitor."

Peter cleared his throat and then changed his mind about adding to the story. "Come on Ice. Let the ladies talk. Sheri needs time to digest all that's happened to her in the last month."

Ice reluctantly put on his coat and grabbed his duffle bag. "I'll call you tomorrow Sheri. Maybe we can talk about this rationally."

Sheri's eyes were clouded over by tears. Johnni hugged her friend and motioned for Ice and Peter to leave.

When the door shut behind them, Sheri burst into tears. "Why is every weirdo in the world after me? What kind of man karma do I have?"

Johnni hugged her friend. "You know Sheri, everything is not always so black and white. Sometimes the universe just hands us something that we don't always understand. I kind of liked the part of seeing his uncle Tony in his plaid leisure suit. Plus, if you think about it, that little dog came into your life and, without knowing you, protected you and almost lost his life. That's a pretty amazing story too."

Sheri sniffed, "But it's crazy. Cleo talking to the dog? Naming him Estupido? Okay, even I have to admit that part is funny. The thing that gets me is he really believes it happened. He believes he was a dog! That's crazy."

Johnni got the giggles. "No, crazy would be if he was trying to lick his balls!"

"Johnni! How can you even joke at a time like this? I can't believe the guy I have been crazy about for most of my life is nuts! I give up."

"No, you are not giving up. You just need a little space to see if there's any truth to this little dog story. I could be wrong but I swear that man is in love with you. But then again, it could just be puppy love. I wonder if his favorite position is doggie style?"

Despite herself, Sheri laughed. "It is kind of funny,

I mean, of all the dogs, the great Ice comes back as a Chihuahua. I'm sure his ego took a hit on that one! Actually, when you think about it, a Chihuahua makes it all a little more believable, especially the part about being called Estupido!"

Both of the women had a good giggle and then Johnni

took her best friend's hands and looked at her . "Sheri, just give him a chance. There are some strange near-death occurrences and by all accounts, he really did almost die. You don't know what happens when they're heading for the bright light.

"Okay, I'll keep an open mind but I'm certainly not talking to him right now. I went ten years. Another few days won't matter."

Johnni sighed. "You are one stubborn girl but I'll let you have this one. You've had enough crazies to last a lifetime. I just don't think that Ice is one of them."

Sheri hugged Johnni and said, "I think it's time for us to make your favorite martini and watch our favorite chick flick."

Johnni threw a sofa pillow at Sheri. "Okay, I'll

watch Sleepless in Seattle for the hundredth time if you promise me you will talk to Ice by the end of the week. If not, I will take your DVD and never watch this movie with you again."

Sheri grimaced. "I promise. But it's only because you threatened Tom Hanks and his cute little boy. I'll talk to him but it doesn't mean he's back in my good graces."

"Girl, it's a start and that's all I'm asking. Now, let's make a couple of martinis and watch your movie."

Chapter 21

Ice was despondent. It had been four days and Sheri still refused to see him or even talk to him on the phone. Peter finally took pity on him. "I'm calling my mom. We need to tell her everything that happened and have her talk to Sheri."

"Your mom would do that for me?"

"No, she'd do it for me. You're driving me nuts and I'm her only son. She won't be able to marry me off if I'm mentally deranged by all this."

Ice threw a shoe at Peter but his smile was from ear to ear. "Okay, let's make that phone call. I haven't seen your mom in years. Is she still as hot-looking?"

"Of all the disgusting things you have ever said, that is the grossest by far. Do not ask me questions like that about my own mother. Dude, show some respect!"

"If I weren't madly in love with Sheri and if your

father didn't look like he could beat the crap out of me, I would totally be her cougar cub." Ice smirked as he saw his friend's face drain of color.

"Ice, if this is the new leaf you're turning over then you're totally screwed. Sheri will never go for a womanizing moron who is going to try and hit on my mom."

"Jeez Arnstrom, what happened to your sense of humor? I love your mother and I would never hit on her. But you can see how young guys become cougar cubs when the older women look like your mom. Really, it's a compliment." Ice was a little confused as to why Peter didn't see things the same way he did.

"Again, please stop. There is no son that wants to hear a guy go on and on about his mother."

Ice started to laugh and then it was like someone threw a bucket of cold water on him. "Peter, do you think your mom can explain things to Sheri?"

"She met Sheri and Johnni at my charity event and liked them both. I'm sure that it will be a woman to woman thing. They'll do some talking, maybe some crying, and in the end, if Britt Louise can't talk sense into them, then no one can."

***

Britt Louise gave Ice an enormous hug. "Jeffrey, we were very worried about you. I'm so happy to see you. Peter says you're thinking of relocating to Seattle. That will give me a chance to put some meat on your bones."

Ice returned the hug and smiled. "Mrs. Arnstrom, I've missed you and your cooking. I still remember the Thanksgiving feast you whipped up for us when we were on the Canadian team. If you can cook such amazing food in a hotel room with a mini kitchen, I can't wait to see what you can do in your own kitchen."

"We'll feed you once we get your problem with Sheri fixed. You boys should have known better. The poor girl has been through hell this past month and then you show up talking the crazy talk."

Peter and Ice started to interrupt and she waved them to silence and continued. "There are some things in life that cannot be explained. I believe that you did come to rescue her as a dog. No one would make up a story about being in a Chihuahua's body." Britt Louise's face lit up in mirth. "Jeffrey, I trust all your equipment is back to normal?"

Ice shot a mortified look at Peter as a blush crept up his face. "You're a dead man, Peter. I can't believe you told her that part."

Peter leaned over and whispered into Ice's ear. "Dude, payback for calling her a hot cougar."

"Boys, I don't have time for all your playing around. I have some cooking to do. I'm taking lunch to Sheri. I've invited Johnni too. Between the three of us, we'll sort this out. Meanwhile, you two behave yourselves."

Cowed, the two men reverted to nine year-old boys as they both mumbled in unison, "Yes ma'm."

Chapter 22

Britt Louise stood on Sheri's front porch carrying two large shopping bags filled with Swedish delicacies. She smiled to herself thinking back to when she fell in love with her husband and the sweet beginnings of new love.

The door opened and Sheri gasped when she saw the amount of food in the bags. "Britt Louise, it's so nice to see you. It looks like you've enough food here to feed an army or a hockey team. You didn't invite Ice over did you?" A look of panic paled her pretty face.

"No dear. I promise it will just be us girls. Is Johnni here yet?" Britt Louise walked in the front door and stopped to take in the room. "Your home is beautiful. The colors are very soothing."

Sheri beamed. "I love this house. I've had it for five years and have done a lot of the work myself. Come see the kitchen. It's my favorite room."

Britt Louise followed at her heels and her smile

widened when she saw the kitchen. "This is beautiful. I can tell you must love to cook. It's perfect."

Sheri's smile faded a bit. "I don' do a lot of cooking for one. Sometimes I have a dinner party or we have girl's night here and make food. It's not being used the way I envisioned it when I had it remodeled."

Britt Louise looked at her with a knowing eye and was about to speak when the front door opened and Johnni called out.

Johnni came into the kitchen and hugged Britt Louise. "I'm so happy you're here. Ohh, what are those wonderful smells? I'm starving."

"We have Swedish meatballs with brown cream sauce, mashed potatoes and lingonberry jam. I also brought pickled gherkins. Swedes love pickles. For dessert we have Pinsesstårta, or as you would say, Princess cake. It's a sponge cake with whipped cream and custard. I thought with all the drama that has been going on, you two deserved a day to be spoiled like Princesses. I know you modern young women don't like the concept of being a princess but allow me to spoil you just for the day."

Sheri looked at the cake longingly. "Princesses always live happily ever after. I just don't see that in my future."

Britt Louise walked over and hugged her. "Don't worry my sweet girl. You'll get your happily-ever-after. But remember, they don't happen unless you trust and believe in the person you love."

Sheri concentrated on making sure the tears didn't fall from her eyes. Johnni saved the day as she hugged Britt Louise. "Spoil away…it won't hurt our feelings.

A half an hour later, the three women sat around the kitchen table enjoying the food. When the three had finished, Britt Louise pulled out a bottle of Swedish punch and a thermos of strong Swedish coffee.

"It's time to talk and I think a little Swedish liquor and coffee will be good." She poured three shot glasses and filled three coffee cups with the strong dark coffee. "It is time for me to tell you a little bit about myself. Sometimes people have certain gifts and you don't question where they came from. You just accept them for how you can use them to help people."

Johnni and Sheri drank their shot and waited for

her to continue.

"In Sweden and in the United States, you have many people that can do what I do. And you have many people that don't believe such a thing is possible. I need you to believe me and keep an open mind. Sheri, could you please go get your cat. Cleo is her name correct?"

Sheri's eyes got big and the penny dropped. She thought all along that the older woman was going to try and get her to forgive Ice for his crazy talk. Now Britt Louise was going to go to crazy town, too.

Noting the look of disbelief on her friend's face, Johnni grabbed her arm. "Girl, you need to keep an open mind and just see where this goes. No harm, no foul."

"Fine, let me go get Cleo. I'm not sure where you're headed with this Britt Louise, but I'll give you the benefit of the doubt."

Sheri went into her bedroom and picked up Cleo who hissed at being woken up from her nap. Carrying her out to the kitchen, she presented her to Britt Louise.

Cleo looked up and grumbled, *why do I have to be woken up from my nap? Oh, wait, I see meatballs. Do I get one?*

"Yes, you do get a meatball."

Cleo jumped up from her lap and went nose to nose with the woman. Frantic meows came out. *You can understand me?*

"Yes I can. Now, I need you to tell me something about Sheri that only you know so she doesn't think I'm a crazy old häxa."

Cleo purred as she looked into Britt Louise's eyes and thought about what to tell her. She put her paw on the older woman's arm and let out a series of meows. Britt Louise laughed with delight. "Really? She googles him everyday?"

Sheri blushed redder than her hair. "What are you talking about? Johnni, did you tell Britt Louise about my cyber stalking?"

"Of course not."

Cleo let out another long litany of meows.

"She says that when Ice was Estupido, he would snuggle next to you and lick your shoulder. Cleo also swears that Ice was Estupido, although she says he really wasn't stupid. And she says that you have your diary from high school hidden under your mattress and sometimes read it after you watch "Sleepless in Seattle." And then you cry."

"Cleo, you stop talking right this minute or I'm taking away all your treats. You little traitor." Sheri had adjusted to having a cat whisperer in her midst. She just needed to shut up the cat that was giving away her secrets.

"I have to give you back something my son took." Britt Louise reached into the sack and pulled out the photo of Ice and Sheri. "He said the little dog brought it to him and he thought maybe I would be able to figure out why. I guess that was Ice trying to tell Peter who he was."

Sheri took the photo and held it close. "I'm happy to have this back. I thought that Pablo had hidden it somewhere."

Britt Louise took Sheri's hand. "I know this is a lot to take in but things happen that cannot be explained. You must have an open mind. I believe Jeffrey was sent here to protect you from the killer. He had some bad karma to work off and that's why he was the teeny tiny dog. But he protected you with everything he had."

"She's right you know." Johnni took Sheri's other hand and gave it a squeeze. "I know you have some thinking to do. I'll tidy up the kitchen. You go for a drive and have some alone time.

Sheri hugged Johnni and Britt Louise. "This is all a lot to take in. I feel like I've fallen down the rabbit hole. I'm going to go think some things through."

Britt Louise clapped her hands together. "Okay, get to it. Johnni and I will take care of everything else."

***

Sheri drove the familiar route to Golden Gardens beach. It was her favorite place in Seattle. The view of the Olympics always cheered her up and now there was new snow glistening off the peaks. It was cold and blustery but, with her down parka and boots, she didn't feel the chill in the air. She sat down on a log and tried to sort out her feelings. Her mind was always driven by facts and figures, not the intangible or unseen. It was a lot to absorb. She had finally arrived at her conclusion when she saw a man with a hoody walking along the beach. She'd know that walk anywhere and actually smiled as she got up and walked over to where he now stood.

"How did you know I'd be here?"

"I didn't. When you brought me here after your lunch with Warren I fell in love with the place. I wanted a place to think about what I was going to do to get you to believe me, or if that didn't work, convince you that I'm not crazy."

Sheri put her arm through his and started walking down the beach. "Oh, you're crazy all right. Always have been, probably always will be. I guess I'm crazy to agree to go out with someone like you, but what the heck….can't hurt to go out on three dates. I've had worse."

Ice had his head down against the wind and thought for a minute he misunderstood. "Wait. Are you saying you're willing to give me a chance?"

"Like I said Zamboni, I've had worse. What do I have to lose?"

Ice had waited long enough. He turned Sheri to face him and gently cupped her face in his gloved hands. He kissed her with such tenderness tears came to her eyes.

He wrapped his arms around her and knew he would never let this woman get away from him again.

Sheri felt his kiss and the promises he made but still wasn't ready to give in. "We'll see Ice Jockey. Try one date and we'll see how it goes."

Ice laughed and kissed her nose. "You're on. Dinner tomorrow night. I'll pick you up at 7:00p.m.

Sheri reluctantly pulled herself out of his arms. "Don't forget to bring some of the Zamboni charm. I still haven't seen any of it."

She turned and walked away. The smile on her face was dazzling and the ice around her heart was starting to thaw.

Chapter 23

Sheri stood in front of her closet staring blankly at the contents. "What am I supposed to wear for a dinner date with Ice Zamboni?"

Johnni was sitting on the bed flipping through a journal detailing shark research in Australia. "Oh, just throw on any old thing. I've seen how that man looks at you. I'm sure he'll rip it off within five minutes."

"Oh no he's not. I told him three dates to see if this thing is going to go anywhere. Sex is off the table for now." Sheri finally locked eyes on the black dress she had worn to the Zodiac bar. "I'm wearing this. Let's see if he recognizes it."

"You look good in that dress. A little nunny but good."

"I do not look like a nun in this dress. Just because

it's not cut down to my navel!" Sheri was used to this argument and continued to get ready for her date.

When the doorbell rang, Sheri looked up to the ceiling and yelled, "Uncle Tony, this is all your fault. This better go well."

Johnni got up to go answer the door and called back to her friend. "That was loud enough to wake the dead, I'm sure he heard you."

Sheri took one final look in the mirror and walked out to meet her date.

When she walked into the room, Ice let out a low wolf whistle, grabbed her into a hug and whispered into her ear. "You look fantastic."

Sheri felt like a teenage girl as a giggle escaped. "Oh my God, I did not mean to do that." She then proceeded to laugh so hard she snorted.

Johnni looked at the couple and let out a laugh of her own. "Okay you two, get on with date number one so we can get this thing started."

Ice let go of Sheri and leaned over to kiss Johnni on the cheek. "Yes Mother. Don't wait up."

***

The Italian Restaurant was cozy and intimate. It was decorated with pictures of Italy on the walls and fake grapes everywhere. Peter had told him to ignore the décor and enjoy the amazing food. As the hostess walked them to their table, her eyes strayed back to Ice every other step. Sheri scooted into the booth and was surprised when Ice sat on her side of the table. She enjoyed the look of disappointment on the hostesses face, thinking to herself how odd it felt to be envied.

"I can't stand to be that far away from you. I love you in this dress. You wore it to the Zodiac Bar the night you made me wear the little Chippendale dancer outfit."

"I'm still kind of wrapping my head around the whole dog thing. Especially since the dog has slept with me and seen me naked. You have an unfair advantage."

Ice's eyes heated up and he said softly, "You can see me naked anytime you want."

Sheri's eyes glazed over. She was thinking how amazing his body looked in clothes but how positively sinful it would look without them. "Not yet, Hockey Boy." Her eyes betrayed her cool words.

Ice leaned over and kissed her lightly on the lips. "You're worth the wait."

When the waiter came, Ice ordered wine and surprised Sheri by ordering dinner for her. Sheri's heart did a little flip flop when she realized he had remembered all of her favorite food and even asked for extra parmesan cheese.

"You remembered my favorite food?"

"It's funny how things like that stick with you. This last month, I've been thinking about a lot of things. Like how you have always been the only person to call me out on my shit."

"Oh yeah….you had a lot of "shit" when we were growing up. I have to ask. How was your prom date with the cheerleader?"

Ice gave a rueful laugh. "So uneventful I don't even remember her name."

"Good. Serves you right." Sheri's smile was wide and her eyes were lit up in amusement. "You know, if we'd gone to prom, you probably wouldn't be here right now."

Ice grabbed her hand. "There are so many things I

would like to go back and change, but if any of it meant I wouldn't be here with you right now, I wouldn't change a thing."

Sheri's eyes glistened with tears and for a second thought she was going to lose it. "What about the time you put the itching powder all over Mr. Haverson's chair? I think you got two weeks of detention for that stunt.

"It was worth it."

They sat in their booth for hours, drinking wine and reminiscing. When the waiter told them the restaurant was closing, they reluctantly left.

"So date number one went well. Want to go for number two?" Ice had his arm around her shoulder and squeezed her in next to him. "You feel good next to me."

Sheri looked up and batted her eyes at Ice. "I guess I could stand one more date with you. What do you have in mind?"

"Lunch tomorrow. I want to do the Space Needle and also the Ferris wheel. The weather forecast says clear skies tomorrow."

"If you stick around, you'll learn not to trust the weather predictions. I'm game. I'm working from home tomorrow so I can clear some time."

Ice drove Sheri home, maneuvering the steering wheel with one hand as he held onto her left hand., unwilling to break the connection even for a moment.

When they arrived at Sheri's house, Ice came around the car to open her door. They walked to the porch hand in hand.

At the front door, Ice pulled Sheri to him and kissed her like a drowning man. He couldn't get enough of her.

Sheri clung to him and kissed him back, matching his intensity with her own. Finally, she gave him a little shove and tried to clear her head of all the carnal thoughts. "Whoa, slow down cowboy. My neighbors are getting quite a show."

Ice gave her one final kiss and walked back to his car. Every cell in his body felt alive and on fire. He turned around just as Sheri was shutting her front door. "Best first date ever. Admit it McLellon. It was for you, too."

In response she blinked the porch light and went off to bed, thinking *oh yeah Hockey Boy, it was.*

***

"Look! Mount Rainier is out! Your weather report was right on. It's a fabulous day to be having lunch in the Needle." Sheri's enthusiasm was contagious.

"What the heck does it mean when you say the mountain is out?" Ice was learning the language of the Northwest.

"We have so many cloudy days here, when it's clear, natives say the mountain is out. Sounded strange to me too at first but when in Rome…"

"I get it. So the Olympic Mountains are on the west side and the Cascades are to the east?"

"Yeah and for mid-November we already have a lot of snow. It's so beautiful here. When I first moved here, I thought the rain would drive me crazy. But the minute the clouds clear and you see the mountains, all is forgiven."

"I'll love it here. Peter wants me to help with his at-risk kid's project and I'm excited to get started. My first day is tomorrow."

Sheri saw the apprehension in his eyes and gave his hand a quick squeeze. "They'll love you. Those boys will figure out really fast that you walk the walk and talk the talk."

Ice laughed and held her hand tight. "As long as you realize I'm walking the walk and talking the talk."

Sheri looked down at her plate and thought how she should answer. When she looked up, she saw the look of naked fear on Ice's face.

"You know how I feel about you, right, McLellon?"

"Ya sure, you betcha." Sheri couldn't resist hitting him with a little Minnesota talk.

"Come on, point out some more stuff." Ice could sense that serious talk was not on the agenda today.

After lunch they made their way to the waterfront and bought tickets for the Ferris wheel. It was a very chilly thirty two degrees and Ice paid extra for the heated car. It was apparent the minute the car ascended up to the top of the Ferris wheel they could generate their own heat.

Ice looked at Sheri as they broke from their kiss.

"I'd say that date number two is in the bag."

Sheri chuckled. "You're pretty smart for a hockey jock. Look how well you can count."

"Oh ye of little faith. I can count way higher than two or three. If I get stuck in the coming years, you can help me keep track."

Ice decided to press his advantage and locked her in a kiss that lasted until the attendant opened the door to their car.

Breathless, Ice handed the kid a fifty and told him to shut the damn door.

***

For the past week, Sheri and Ice had brought new meaning to the term "speed dating." Date three was a Seahawks game. Ice had seats at the fifty yard line and watched Sheri in the media booth. After she wrapped up her post-game interviews, they went to dinner and discussed the game and the player's stats. It was a page from their past, having had similar discussions so many times. It felt so right to rekindle that competitive edge, trying to out-do each other with their knowledge of player stats.

When she got home, Sheri called Johnni. Ice's goodbye kiss had made her weak at the knees and her voice was a little breathless.

"OMG, you are out of breath. Did you just have sex with Ice?"

"No. I told you I'm waiting to see how this goes. This was date number three. I have no idea if I'll see him again." Sheri almost cried out those words.

"You sound upset. Do you want me to come over?" Johnni jumped out of bed and pulled a pair of jeans from her closet.

"I'm okay. But here's the thing. If he dumps me I'm taking all my black dresses and joining a nunnery. God, I can't believe in just three dates I'm a goner." Sheri choked back a sob. "I love him dammit. What if he breaks my heart again?"

"Sheri, I've seen the way he looks at you. He's just been waiting for you to catch up to where he's been for the last two months. Actually, I think he's loved you for a long time and figured it out when he was the purse puppy."

"It'd be so much easier if he still was a purse puppy.

I'll talk to you tomorrow. I'm going to cuddle up to Cleo and figure out how I can take her with me when I become a nun."

The last noise Sheri heard before hanging up was Johnni's hoots of laughter.

Chapter 24

It was time. Tonight was their fourth date and Ice took a look around Peter's guest room as he picked up his gift for Sheri. He hoped he had just spent his last night at Peter's house.

As he rang the bell, he said a silent prayer to his Uncle Tony. *Please tell the Big Guy to give me some help tonight.*

Sheri answered the door and looked down at the duffel bag in his hand. "Hey Hockey Boy, what's in the bag? Did you bring your jammies thinking you'd get lucky?"

"No, I brought you a present."

"Really?" As Sheri looked down, Ice spied Cleopatra making her grand entrance.

"Cleo baby. Get your bad cat ass in here. I have

something I think you'll like."

Just then, a yelp startled them both and Cleo let out a hiss.

"Oh hell no, you did not bring what I think you did." Cleo's snarly meows were loud and threatening.

Sheri opened up the duffel bag with a mesh end, the male version of the puppy purse. A small black and white Chihuahua puppy with enormous ears and eyes stared up at her. Scared to death after hearing the growls from Cleo, the puppy was shaking.

"Ice, what have you done? Look at this little guy. He's adorable. You know Cleo will never accept him." As she spoke, she put him in her lap and looked down. Cleo jumped up on the sofa, ready to pounce when she saw the tiny shaking puppy.

"Oh my, you are a teeny tiny puppy." Cleo figured out immediately that this little creature was no threat and her maternal instinct came out. *"Well, it has been kind of lonely since Estupido left."*

The puppy looked up and said *"Momma?"*

Sheri looked at Ice. "What are they saying?"

"I think it's going to be okay. I've noticed that my

ability to understand what Cleo is saying is getting harder. I can't understand her words anymore, just her feelings.. It looks like my evil plan is going to work. Look, she likes the puppy."

Sheri arched her eyebrow in question. "Your evil plan?"

Ice got down on one knee. "Sheri, I want more than three dates…..I want three million dates with you. I want a lifetime. I want you to see this puppy as testament of my commitment."

It was then that Sheri noticed the ring hanging from a red ribbon tied to the puppy's collar.

"I love you Sheri. Marry me. I promise I will cherish you for the rest of my life. I'm not complete without you."

Sheri tried to process everything that had happened in the last three minutes. She looked down at the little **puppy snoring so**ftly as he laid next to Cleo, who was giving him a bath. Her world had just been turned upside down.

"Come on McLellon, marry me. I love you more than hockey. That's got to mean something."

"Wow, more than hockey?" Sheri paused a moment and tears slipped from her eyes. "Yes. Yes I'll marry you and yes, I love you more than hockey too."

"Really?" Ice picked her up and twirled her around. He finally stopped, took the ribbon from the puppy's neck and slipped the ring on her finger. "I am the luckiest man in the world."

"You've got that right, Hockey Boy." Sheri looked down at her hand and then into Ice's eyes. "I have to admit, I never thought I'd be thankful that a serial killer was after me. It brought you here, and for that, I'll be thankful the rest of my life."

Ice hugged Sheri close to him. "My uncle Tony was right. My life was going nowhere without you."

Sheri looked down at the puppy and Cleo. "What's the puppy's name?"

"I was thinking of naming him Mark Antony but we'll call him Tony."

"You want to name the dog after your dead uncle?"

"No. I want to name him after Cleopatra and Mark Antony, the greatest love story in history. That is, until we became the greatest love story."

Sheri smiled and grabbed the front of Ice's shirt. "About that love story. It's time for me to get a look at you naked, and, if you play your cards right, I might even lick your shoulder. After all, turn-about is fair play."

Cleopatra looked on as Ice swept Sheri into his arms and carried her to the bedroom. She heard the door shut firmly behind them and did a little cat smile. As much as she hated to share Sheri, she thought about the puppy and Ice joining their household and felt content as she snuggled into little Tony.

She could hear loud moans coming from the bedroom and felt the puppy start to shake. *"Momma, what are those loud noises?"*

Cleo gave him a good lick and responded. *"Baby boy, those are the sounds of happily ever after."*

Please take a moment to write a review on Amazon; your feedback is always appreciated.

A little about the Author

I grew up in Seattle and for the past 25 years have lived a little east of Seattle in Renton with my husband, Gary Arnold, our German Shepherd, Jetta and orange/blonde tabby cat, Mojo. I love living in the Pacific Northwest, surrounded by mountains and water. When winter comes, we pack up our motor home, with the animals and head south. Maybe living in a forty foot motor home with an eighty-two pound dog and a ten pound cat is where the crazy dialog started for this book. I swear they talk to each other and I'm sure their language is "R" rated!

Writing has become a late in life passion. An avid reader, I always wanted to write a book "someday." I'm glad retirement has given me the opportunity to pursue my dream. This is my first attempt at a romantic comedy. My two other books are historical fiction, **'The Good Deed'** and the sequel, **'The Misdeed'** available in print and Kindle version.

Here's an excerpt from *The Good Deed*

Chapter 1
Ireland - 1920

Edward O'Brien and Lydia Delaney had not spoken in four years, much to the delight of her younger sister, Myra, who had her heart set on the boy. When Edward O'Brien was ten years old, his dream was to marry Lydia Delaney. He fell in love with her, and to prove it, pushed her into a mud puddle. His fate was sealed when she screamed after him, "I hate you Edward O'Brien and I'll not speak to you ever again!"

That proclamation lasted until Lydia was fourteen and suddenly saw Edward through new eyes. The ten year old menace had grown into a tall young man with broad shoulders. His boyish face had become masculine with a hint of whiskers starting above his upper lip. Edward's contagious smile lit up his face and made his sky blue eyes dance with merriment. His slightly crooked nose kept his face from being too perfect. Lydia regretted ignoring him for four years.

Lydia spent days trying to get in front of Edward, but to no avail. She would spot him in the hallway, but he was always surrounded by his friends. She wasn't about to approach him at school.

As punishment from Father O'Reilly for failing a religion test, Edward had to serve early Mass for two weeks giving, Lydia her chance. Edward watched Lydia kneeling at the communion rail. Her beautiful blue eyes closed as Father O'Reilly stood in front of her ready to give the Communion Host. Edward's anger flared as he thought of how she had refused to speak to him for the last four years. He mused to himself as he held the silver tray beneath her chin; *she's a lassie that doesn't forget, stubborn as the day is long.* Father O'Reilly placed the host on her tongue, and Edward watched her full lips curve into a smug smile when she peeked up and saw him staring at her.

He looked down at her clear porcelain skin; the faint smattering of freckles across her nose reminded him of the ten year old he had been so in love with. Her heart-shaped face looked innocent as she crossed herself after swallowing the Host. A pretty blush lit up her face, and she glanced at Edward before turning to walk back to her pew. He was thinking how beautiful she looked and a pang of longing hit his heart. Father O'Reilly moved on to the next parishioner while Edward silently followed, not noticing the malevolent looks directed at Lydia, by her younger sister, from the back of the church.

Every morning Lydia showed up for Mass, taking communion, getting braver each day, opening her eyes and smiling at Edward as the priest put the host on her tongue. She lingered after Mass hoping to catch him as he came out of the church, but Edward always ducked out the rear door to meet up with his friends before school. Neither of them noticed Myra hiding in the back of the church, watching their every move.

He only had three more days of early Mass. He walked out the front of the church after changing into his school clothes. Sauntering out as if he had no cares in the world, Edward saw Lydia dawdling by the door. He passed her by without a look and Lydia called after him.

"Edward O'Brien, where are your manners? Are you too good to be sayin' hello to a classmate?" Her tone was huffy and it annoyed Edward.

"You have not spoken to me in four years? Why on earth waste time saying hello to someone who won't respond?" Edward couldn't contain his anger. "I'll be saying hello to you," he continued, "when you can be cordial and let bygones be bygones. It was four years ago that I pushed you. Why haven't you gotten over it by now?"

"Well, most people would have had the courtesy to apologize for pushing someone into the mud for no reason.

The manners you lack are not my fault." Lydia turned and stomped off.

Edward spent the day at school pondering the situation. Lydia refused to look at him but he was used to it. Being ignored for four years had inured him to her stubbornness, but now, with a chance to make up, he was at a loss.

He walked over to his sister's house after school. Rosie was twelve years older, married with two children, and his favorite sister. As he walked up the stairs to the porch, his head down and shoulders slumped in misery, Rosie looked out the window.

Ah, this should be good, she thought. Her mother had sent word through the family telegraph system that Edward had been acting strangely and feared her youngest child was having trouble at school. Rosie looked at her young brother's handsome face and realized he was growing up, a far cry from the young bairn she used to bathe and change his nappies. He was a burgeoning young man and the look on his face screamed girl trouble.

Rosie was the beauty of the family. Her strawberry blonde hair and emerald green eyes were the calling card of the O'Briens. At least one woman in each generation inherited those features. Edward looked at his nephew who had Rosie's hair and his niece who had her eyes. Edward laughed in spite of himself thinking, *she'll probably have four or five more. She's bound to get the combination correct at some point.*

"What brings you by?" She quickly added, "Not that I'm not overjoyed to see my baby brother, mind you. I could use a little break from my day. Let's have a bit of tea and a biscuit."

Following her into the kitchen, Edward could contain himself no longer. "I should never have pushed her."

Alarmed, Rosie grabbed him by the shoulders. "You pushed a girl? Who did you push?"

"Lydia Delaney. I pushed her into a mud puddle and she hasn't spoken to me in four years, and now she wants to and I want her to, but she got mad all over again, and I don't know how to fix it." His words rushed out in a tumble and Rosie did her best not to smile.

"Why did you push her? And why am I just hearing about it now?" Rosie was the oldest of ten children and by the time Edward had come along, their mother was too exhausted to worry about another child. Rosie had raised Edward until she married four years ago and moved into her own home. "Did you push her because you were mad at me for getting married and leaving you?"

In her mind it seemed logical, but logic flew out the

245

window as Edward proclaimed. "I pushed her in the mud because I loved her and knew I was going to marry her someday."

Rosie realized at ten, a boy pushing a girl in the mud was as good as a proposal and bit the inside of her cheeks to stifle her laughter. "All right now. So she hasn't spoken to you in four years? She is one unforgiving young lady. Are you sure this is the love of your young life?"

"Rosie, if you make fun of me I'll leave right now!" Edward's frustration was becoming more evident. It was time to start fixing this mess.

"All right, my sweet Eddie, let me see if I understand. You love her, you pushed her in the mud to prove it, she stopped talking to you, now she wants to talk to you and you want to talk to her, so tell me now, why are you here and not talkin' to the lass?"

"She got mad at me and said I never apologized to her. I didn't see the point since she swore never to speak to me again and now it's too late."

"Well four years is a bit of a delay for an apology, but it looks like it is the only thing to get you out of this mess. Eddie, be a man and offer a sincere apology or give up on her altogether."

"But, Rosie, the whole school will laugh at me."

Edward was becoming more distressed, thinking he'd look a fool in front of his friends.

"Eddie, pick some flowers, put on clean clothes, go over to her house, and ask her to forgive you. But be warned. If you start with this young girl and she is this stubborn, you'll have to cater to her forever." Rosie was worried helping Edward with this girl might be a big mistake, but the pitiful look on his face made her hold back further words of warning. *God help me if she breaks his heart someday, it will be my fault.*

୧

The next day was Saturday. With no school and his chores done, Edward proceeded to get cleaned up in his Sunday clothes. Dark hair slicked back, sneaking a bit of his da's aftershave lotion after shaving the fuzz above his upper lip, Edward started off on the long walk to Lydia's home. "Why does she have to live on the other side of the village?" He grumbled as he walked along. "God help me if I run into any of my friends seeing me all dressed up and carrying flowers."

Edward continued his desolate march finally arriving at Lydia's door and making a tentative knock. Then, in a moment of anger at the predicament he was in, knocked loudly. "Lydia, come out. If it's an apology you want, I'm here to make it."

Lydia had been watching his approach from her upstairs window. She could tell by his stride he was working himself into a temper. Descending the stairs, she heard her ma coming down the hall to answer the door. She called out, "It's for me, Ma. I'll get the door." Holding her breath and wondering what Edward would say, Lydia slowly opened the front door.

"Well, it's about time. You waited four years for this. I guess you're in no big hurry."

"Did you come here to have another fight? Maybe you'd like me to come outside and find some mud to push me into?" Lydia couldn't stop the words from coming out.

"All right, I'll say what I've come to say. I'm sorry I pushed you all those many years ago. You were just so beautiful and all the other boys were looking at you. I knew I wanted you to be mine so I pushed you in the mud to show you how I felt." Edward was stammering but bravely continued. "I thought you knew I liked you. I never thought you could be so cruel and not speak to me for four long years. So here's my apology. I'm sorry. I'm sorry I pushed you. I'm sorry I made you so mad. I'm sorry I yelled at you the other day, and I'm sorry your flowers are wilted from my long walk. There, I'm done apologizing."

Lydia smiled, deep dimples creasing her cheeks. "I accept your apology, and I'm sorry I didn't speak to you for four years, but how was I supposed to know you liked me?" Lydia was doing the best she could to curb her tongue and not tell him what an idiot he was. But then, she caught sight of the distress in his face and her heart softened. "Edward, it's a beautiful day. Let me put these flowers in water, and we'll walk down the lane together for a spell."

Edward waited at the door as she took the flowers from his outstretched hand and went to find a vase. Coming back, she grabbed a jumper from the hook by the door and closed it behind her. Lydia shyly took Edward's hand, and they headed down the lane while from the upstairs window, eyes an identical clear blue like Lydia's, turned green with envy as her older sister strolled down the lane with the only boy Myra ever wanted. Going to the closet, Myra picked up Lydia's favorite dress and stabbed it with sewing scissors until it was a useless rag.

ACKNOWLEDGEMENTS:

Thank you to my husband, Gary Arnold, my family, and my friends for their encouragement.

I am grateful for the proofreading skills of Ro Burnham, Lynne Milnor and Rick North. To my writing group, Kathleen Lawrence, Ed Nichols, Mark Bowman, Bart Bardeleben, and Susan Schrieber, thank you for your feedback and thoughts.

Made in the USA
Middletown, DE
17 November 2019